THE
BADASS WITCH

A Romance Novel About the Power of a Woman

Will she be awarded the CEO position she's worked so hard for, or will attraction get in the way of her success?

||| | | |||||||||| |||||| |||| |||
I0659151

By EXCELLUS O. HYLAND

Imprint of Excelland Publishing

ISBN: 978-1-7378434-0-5 (Paperback)
ISBN: 978-1-7378434-1-2 (Ebook)

Front cover image by Kamaljeet Singh
Book design by Kamaljeet Singh

Printed the United States of America.

Disclaimer: The publisher and the authors do not make any guarantee or other promise as to any results that may be obtained from using the content of this book. This publication is meant as a source of valuable information for the reader, however it is not meant as a substitute for direct expert assistance. If such level of assistance is required, the services of a competent professional should be sought.

Dedication

I would like to dedicate this book to Janelle Monae. Your words of inspiration and support is what ignited the spark within me and as a result my dreams of becoming an author has come true.

Acknowledgement

This is a work derived from and inspired by many women I have encountered in my life but a few of which I specify my thanks to now. I am grateful to Sergeants M. Miller and K. White, two badass witches—thanks for allowing me to get to this point in life. Sherria Fowles—thanks for the calls that kept me in tune with society and sane. And Dinah—thanks for giving me a bunk in the shelter and being, how you say, my first girlfriend.

To my editor, Dara Powers Parker—thanks for the meticulous editing services you provided, for taking my masterpiece to another level, and for realizing my potential. A special thank you goes to Reea Rodney at Dara Publishing, LLC. The God and grace in you allowed the rebirth of this work. I'm thankful for your knowledge in publishing—you know your stuff, just like Gwendolyn.

And speaking of Gwendolyn, I would like to thank the namesake of my protagonist, who will forever be my future.

Thanks to my Sister/Mama Tiffany "Tinky" Royal and Sandy Hyland-Hugue. To my niece Olivia Hugue—I love seeing you strive everyday, not a victim of gun violence but a survivor; you are my "Shero" and motivation as of late. And thanks to my other wonder-nieces Algeria and Angela Royal; Theresa Davis, who lives to be more everyday—I love your go power; and my Auntie Latrisa Tuff-Nunnally—our talks be spiritual—love you, woman.

A special thanks to my cousin Lorra Hyland, and last but not the least, my cousin and guiding star Tonja Nunnally—you have been my gas for this journey, #waiting2excel.

Badass Love and #tobecontinued… My writing career is just the beginning. There's more to come.

witch, n. an intelligent, outspoken, ambitious, and bold woman

badass, adj. tough, uncompromising, or intimidating;
n. a formidably impressive or tough person

Prologue

Ancient Egypt

The god's bedchamber was decked out with fine silks from eastern China and solid gold ornaments. The bed was stuffed with a zillion peacock feathers, giving it a softness that compared to floating in air, and the pillows were also peacock feathers encased in silk. The bedpost was made of fine gold, trimmed with diamonds and other gems.

The room was spacious, at least 6,000 square feet. A master bedroom of the grandest mansion could fit in the god's bedchamber, and the bed was the lavish centerpiece.

Eyes closed in a magnificent slumber, the god fluffed his pillow as he lay in his luxurious bed, then instinctively reached out to his wife. He felt only the fine silk bedspread.

He opened his eyes to see the obvious. His wife was not in bed. *Where could she be?* he thought.

The god sat up in bed, considering whether or not to seek out his wife. He had a *foreboding* feeling. No, it was not a foreboding because there had been trouble in his world, his goddom. It wasn't trouble to come; the trouble was already here.

This thought made his blood chill, then the thought and feeling combined into a realization. He realized that it was his blood that was causing him such grief. He knew that he and his wife were in danger.

Yes, it would be best to check on his wife, the beautiful goddess, his pride and joy. He knew his enemy was aware of what a prize his wife was and would not hesitate to harm her to get to him.

He rose out of the bed, slipping on his sandals. He wore no gown, only the custom leather belt with thick, long leather strips that extended to his mid-thigh in the front and back, covering his private parts but exposing his dark hips.

He walked regally toward the large twin doors in search of his wife. But as he reached them, they burst open. The god, startled, stumbled back as a group of men dressed in ancient Egyptian battle armor rushed inside the bedchamber.

The men wore similar armor as his warriors. Assuming that they were his, and more than ready to reprimand them for violating his privacy by bursting into in his bedchamber without formally announcing their presence, he boomed, "What is the meaning of this?" in his Aramaic tongue.

The warriors remained ominously silent standing before him—no, they stood *around* him, brandishing spears and swords. He could not help but feel surrounded, and this more than worried him.

He took a step back, and the warriors stepped forward, closing in on him.

"I am your god, Osiris! Stand down," he ordered in a quivering tone.

The warriors lowered their weapons. *They obeyed,* he thought with relief. But just as quickly as his relief came, it left when he saw who walked in.

"Set!" he cried out.

Set was his brother and "immortal enemy." He appeared in all his glory, donning a special-made purple robe draped in a rainbow of jewels with some ostentatious leather-strapped sandals that made his already imposing height more dominating. Standing six feet, six inches tall, his dark skin glistened like polished charcoal. The muscles that protruded from his neck to his calves looked as solid as rock.

"Seize him!" Set ordered the warriors.

Two of the warriors with swords took hold of Osiris with their free arms and raised their swords to his neck, piercing his flesh. Osiris, standing as tall as his brother and mirroring his muscular structure, did not resist.

"You are no longer the ruler of Egypt, my frail brother," Set told him. "Take him away and cut him into pieces. For on this day, I have cut my mighty brother down from his assumed position."

"No!" Osiris exclaimed.

The warriors carried Osiris out. He halfheartedly squirmed in the warriors' grip. They unremorsefully plunged their swords through his throat. Osiris's blood sprayed from his wounds over all the men present. He thought he was sure to die, and he felt every ounce of blood flow out of him.

Osiris felt his vitality diminishing. He felt the piercing of his flesh, the slicing of skin, as one would imagine the pain and fear of a sacrificial lamb when the high priest slit its throat. Was he a sacrifice for Set to be blessed with his godly rule?

"Take him to the dungeon at once," Set commanded. Osiris felt himself dragged away. His sandals came off, causing his feet to scrape against the hard clay floor and another pain to coincide with the sting in his throat.

As his feet dragged, his nails and flesh ripped away, and he could not help but wonder how it was that he never knew the pyramid castle had a dungeon. Maybe it was such a mundane, lowly retreat that he never bothered to attend or inspect. Now he would be an attendant, and he was certain to be familiarized with it and its captivity.

After rough escort, he arrived at his destination—the Dungeon.

The dungeon was one of many secret storage rooms that archaeologists would discover thousands of years later. Osiris was placed on an elevated stone block, a prehistoric version of an operating table. The warriors gathered after laying the god out on the table. Flat on his back, he began choking on his blood and raising up in convulsive spasms.

The warriors, standing on opposite sides of Osiris, laid their weapons down and pressed the god down on the table. Osiris struggled underneath their grip—not out of resistance, but agonizing pain. He ceased for a moment, and the warriors retrieved their weapons.

Osiris, with his upper torso and feet raised in flying bird fashion, saw the warriors going for their weapons. He stared in horror as they raised their swords. One of the warriors brought down his sword on Osiris's right shoulder, at the joint where the arm connected, and began hacking and sawing at the god's arm, as another warrior did the same on the other side.

"AHLL, OHLAHL!" Osiris screamed. He could feel every gnawing cut of flesh and bone. The pain was excruciating.

His heartbeat accelerated rapidly. He did not know how long it would be until his heart exploded. He hated to think about it, let alone feel it. He silently willed them to cut his head off next to disconnect him from the pain and suffering of his body.

The warriors proceeded to butcher Osiris, whose heart finally stopped beating when they castrated him, cutting off his testicles as well. Although, he had probably lost his testicles figuratively as soon as his brother had overthrown him.

The warriors then placed his body parts in a wool sack. Without bothering to cleanse themselves of the blood that drenched them, they proceeded to take the remains to Set.

Set was inside his new residence as the ruling god of Egypt when the blood-spattered warriors arrived, toting the sack together, for the dead weight of Osiris's body parts was heavy.

"Spread his remains across the Nile River," Set ordered. The men turned to do as they were told.

*   *   *

Osiris's wife, who was gathering incense and pomegranates with three of her nymphs in the beautiful gardens of Cush in Ethiopia, was approached by a slave messenger on a camel. The slave seemed to be in a hurry and looked as if he had been running for his life. The camel's tongue was as dry as the sand in Egypt, and it looked as if it were ready to tilt over and die of exhaustion.

"ISIS! ISIS!" the slave exclaimed. Isis and all the nymphs, clothed in cream dresses and flowery headdresses, turned to the slave. "ISIS! ISIS!" he exclaimed again.

Isis, a goddess of even temperament, became a little agitated by the repetitive proclamation of her name, as if she did not know who she was.

"Speak," she said. Isis was not the type to waste breath on supercilious words, even if she were dealing with a mad man.

The slave breathed in and out, gathering himself as if he were the one having been ridden miles and miles in the scorching heat.

"Lordess, Osiris has been murdered," he finally said.

The breath escaped the goddess, and she could not speak.

"Set has occupied the pyramid castle and proclaimed himself god of Egypt," he informed her.

Isis knew that Set's grievance with his brother was legendary in Egypt—a sibling rivalry as accursed as that of Cain and Abel—Set being the dark moon of his brother Osiris the Sun.

"He," the slave continued, "is awaiting your return to claim you as his wife, and he is prepared to kill you if you refuse him."

The goddess knew her brother-in-law's envy of his brother included the coveting his wife. She was the completion of his life's goal. However, she had no intention of being married to Set.

"Where is my husband's body?"

The question took the messenger aback, but then he thought a moment and said, "My Lordess, I hate to inform you, but the god's body has been cut up into pieces and spread down the Nile."

Isis frowned. "Nymphs."

"Yes, my Lordess," the three nymphs said in unison.

"Prepare my camel and my bag," she told them.

"Yes, my Lordess," the nymphs stammered, scurrying off to do as they were told. The hesitation in their response was not from the goddess's odd request for a camel for traveling (instead of her slaves who pulled her carriage) but from her bag. Isis's bag was allegedly filled with magic, the source of her godly powers.

"You are dismissed," she said to the messenger, who cowered at the mention of the goddess's legendary bag.

When the camel and bag were ready, Isis instructed her nymphs to remain in Cush until her return and to prepare a pentagram with five candles and burn incense. They nodded and left.

Before saddling up, she reached in her bag and pulled out a beaded necklace. Instead of wearing it around her neck, she kept it in her hand, unconsciously rubbing it with her thumb.

"Lead me to you, my love," she said. Then she harnessed the bag onto the camel and mounted it. When she reached the Nile River, she felt herself moving toward its edge. When she got there, she found Osiris's left arm, with his wedding ring still on his finger, lying in the mud alongside the river.

She dismounted the camel and reached in her bag, pulling out a folded wool sack. She placed the arm inside. She gathered the sack and led her camel to a loose stone where she tied the reins. Then she proceeded down the Nile River to retrieve the rest of her husband's body parts. After his left arm, she found his right leg and right arm, left leg, then Osiris's torso, and finally his head, next to his penis and testicles.

Isis stared at his face when she found his head lying on its side, eyes open and looking off in the distance. She picked it up and cradled it after dusting it off. The goddess was hurt to see her god like this. A mighty tear dropped from her eye, then two slow streams flowed down the sides of her face.

Isis held out Osiris's head to face her, raised it up to her face, and kissed him on his full lips. Holding his head away, she inspected his features. His cheek bones still had their luster, his prominent nose still defined his African traits, aligned with his oval eyes with their glassy, black pupils staring blankly, yet seeming to be aware of her. The life in his eyes—the fire—was not present. Isis was used to this impassive look, as he had worn it even when he was alive.

She shook her head slowly and walked back to the sack, which she had sat next to the river. She placed the head inside, closed the sack, and heaved it over her left shoulder. She took two heavy steps from the weight of her dead husband. Nevertheless, she was determined to carry on, so she took a few exaggerated breaths and began walking toward her camel. Then she remembered his private parts and went back to retrieve them.

By the time Isis got back, darkness had fallen on the earth, leaving enough light to illuminate the moon and specks of forming stars. The nymphs, when they spotted her far away, ran ahead to her to assist her. Isis handed down the wool sack. One of the nymphs tried to lift the sack, but Isis shook her head.

"Laquisha, Latifah. Help Latasha."

They all took hold of the sack. Straining from the unexpected heavy weight, they understood why Isis told them to help each other. But what they could not understand was how the petite goddess was able to balance the weight on top of the camel, or how she had even managed to hoist it and herself up there in the first place.

"Place it where you put the pentagram," she said. Isis dismounted the camel as the nymphs, struggling, carried the sack through the gardens. She grabbed her bag and followed them. They walked to a flat surface that bordered the field. A few steps from the field, candles lit up the night. The candles crowned every point of the pentagram.

The nymphs dropped the sack outside of the pentagram. Isis inspected the pentagram, nodded her approval, then said, "Leave me be." The nymphs scurried off.

Isis dropped her bag next to the sack. Then she kneeled and opened the sack, spilling out its contents. Osiris's body parts tumbled out on the ground. She placed the beaded necklace inside her bag and pulled out a jar filled with white powder. She lifted it to her face, inspecting it. Satisfied with what she saw, she nodded and put it down. Then she picked up one of Osiris's arms and placed it inside the pentagram, followed by the rest of his body parts. *Done.* She bent down to retrieve the jar.

Jar in hand, she plucked out its cork stopper and poured out a handful of powder. She kneeled over Osiris's body parts and looked up in the sky, locking onto that ominous star that aligned with the moon. Looking down to her open palm, she blew the powder over Osiris's body parts until they were sprinkled.

The flames on the candles flickered and rose before subsiding. Out of the joints sprouted long wormy veins, seeking out the limbs they were once attached to. When they connected, the limbs slowly knit together, miraculously sealing themselves with flesh with a precision that not even a master surgeon could have sown and leaving no noticeable scars.

Osiris was whole again.

"Wake up!" Isis commanded. Osiris coughed and gasped for air, as if he had been rescued from drowning. Then, he sat upright. Isis had no need for incantations or chants, as the witches after her would, although she did have frankincense and myrrh burning and the candles and pentagram for invoking Osiris and commanding him to take ownership of his body.

Isis fixed him with a stern glare. Osiris peered into his wife's dark eyes as if mesmerized.

"You are the god, Osiris, ruler of Egypt," she reminded him. "You have not acted like a god since the start of the war between you and your little brother." She emphasized the word *little*. "You know you have an army as well as he does, so why don't you fight?"

Osiris considered his wife's words that seemed to roar as a mighty thunder.

"Remember who you are—who you sought to be, and who you were born to be."

He was a god, he knew. A ruler. So why had he been quivering in his sandals for so long? It had been ridiculous. His wife's words resonated.

"Now go out there and defeat your enemy," Isis said.

Osiris rose to his feet with a newfound fire that surged through him, heating him up like the sun. He regretted his past inaction and was determined to act now. He ran off into the night to do as his wife said— defeat his enemy.

To be continued…

Chapter 1

Modern-day Miami, Florida

Gwendolyn Thompson was one of five hundred employees at Armedia, Inc., a global technology company. She was assigned to the sales and marketing of the variety of products the company manufactured or distributed. Her job was really two jobs, but she wasn't being compensated accordingly. The company bled her of her talent and potential.

Just last earning period, she'd made the company millions of dollars and saved them even more. Nonetheless, she was not even rewarded for her outstanding work. Gwendolyn was not bitter, though. She more so saw her job as a steppingstone to bigger and better things. She planned to one day own her own business or take over the one she worked for. It was possible, and she knew enough about the business to take it on. It was just a matter of time before she did.

Gwendolyn sat in her office—at least they gave her her own office—with the usual stack of papers and a computer ready to be fed invoices and payables. The work was easier than it appeared, though, especially with the newest software that already provided the forms. All she needed to do was type in the necessary information, and the paperwork was what she had already deduced or prepared. She was familiar enough with the program to knock down the stack before she was due to clock out, which was at five o'clock. It was now 3:30 p.m.

She had the papers ready to present to the sales team that showed this fiscal year's successful profits. Yes, she was pretty much the reason Armedia, Inc. was profitable. Armedia engaged in the sale of telecommunication devices and other such gadgets. The corporation also owned a few radio stations and a nice share of a television network.

The licensing and purchasing of programs were part of Gwendolyn's job as well. She could be doing better numbers but knew the CEO position was up for grabs. She made it her business to buy a good amount of stock in the company whenever she could, even when Disney was dominating the market. She wanted to have more incentives in case she ever was promoted to CEO—the usual stock options awarded would not be appealing.

As a result, they would have to offer the pay raise that should extend to eight figures a year, which was what she deserved. That would make her the highest paid woman CEO in the world, and at thirty-six, the youngest head of a billion-dollar corporation.

Head down, pen and highlighter in hand, Gwendolyn was working on her papers when there was a knock on her door. She ignored it. Then there was a repeated knock, followed by an echoing double knock.

This mothafucka's persistent, she thought in annoyance. She hated to be disturbed when she started on her work. She was slightly OCD in that she had to see a task to its completion—no interruptions. When she started on a project, her determination to see it through to the end bordered on obsession.

"Who is it?" she managed to ask in a polite tone.

"Trent," came the reply.

Mr Frazier was the supervisor, chief marketing officer (CMO) and, how she viewed it, her saboteur. She hated him to no end. He was obnoxious, inconsiderate, ungrateful, and unpleasant in both manners and looks. She wanted to tell him she was busy—"Go the fuck away"—but acting on impulse was the equivalent of the Dave Chapelle show skit, "When Keepin' It Real Goes Wrong." Gwendolyn could hear the deep voice of the commentator now: "Gwen could put on airs and answer her supervisor whom she couldn't stand by politely answering his knock and commence to her life and career goals. Or she could keep it real!"

"Gwen could tell his ass off and say a thing or two about how she feels and lose her job, probably be forced to work a job beneath her, and reduced to welfare assistance and a lifetime of embarrassment. Which is when keepin' it real goes wrong."

"Come in," she said, taking the high road. Some people were not worth it, and Mr. Trent was one of these people. Mr. Trent walked in wearing a tacky pinstripe suit, his usual, with an even tackier tie.

"Gwen—" he started, but she cut him off.

"With all due respect, sir, please address me in a formal manner." He had the tendency to try to call her by her first name, implying an intimacy that she did not want with him.

"Uhm-uhm, excuse me, Ms. Thompson," he corrected, making her feel good about checking his ass. "I came to ask whether or not you were finished with the presentation for the tele-camera?"

Gwendolyn had been put to task to develop a comprehensive promo for the latest device they were developing, a professional camera that also functioned as a telephone. However, at the present, the camera phone could only call another tele-camera. How was such a device worth consumers' money, she had no idea. This is how she knew the sabotaging characteristic she attributed to Mr. Trent was on point because this product should not be sold by Armedia, or any company.

It made no sense to an average Joe—probably a few photographers, but "a few" was not what the company was in business for. Going global was the idea. So, by presenting such an obvious failure to the masses, it would tank. Then she gets the blame for it, giving her a black eye when being considered for promotion.

And, if it prospers, *he* gets the credit. But she had a trick up her sleeve for him.

"Yes, sir. However, I don't plan to put it on the market until summertime," she told him. Summer was not for another six months. By then she planned to have another viable excuse prepared, eventually forcing him to can the idea or getting the higher-ups to do so.

"Why summertime?" he asked.

"Because the summer is when people tend to go on outings and use their cameras. Sometimes, while out snapping photos, they might need to make a call. For instance, a family on a camping trip decides to split up to take competing photos. They could communicate with each other on their whereabouts and brag about the images they've captured."

Mr. Trent rubbed his unkempt goatee—a stringy, reddish blond lineage of dirty wool. He nodded. "That's brilliant, Ms. Thompson."

She knew when she outlined the quality and effect of the product, she would trick him into putting his name behind the frivolous device that made no damn sense to her. She did not care if it prospered or not, as long as she would not have to bear the burden of its outcome.

"I thought you would like it, sir," she said in the subservient tone he expected from her. As a woman, and a Black one at that, she was aware that men in the workplace thought they were in control and that women were supposed to be glad they had them to rule over them. But Gwendolyn couldn't care less what men thought when she knew what she knew.

"I do, I do," he said. She could practically see the rusted wheels of thought in his head turning. "Very well. I'll leave you to it."

"Thank you, sir," she said, noting that he did not ask for a precise date or to see her presentation. Knowing the conniving bastard, he probably planned to backdoor her and come out with the product himself.

She mentally shrugged it off as a never mind. "Bye, sir," she said, in case he felt obligated to make small talk before his departure, or worse, try to hit on her.

"Okay, I'll be off," he said in a pompous tone. He tried to act like he had an upper-class upbringing, but Gwendolyn knew better. He was not anything but a dirty hick trying to be more than he was. She didn't say anything else and, to emphasize the dismissal, peered down at her paperwork.

Mr. Trent let himself out but left her door open. She sighed and got up to close the door but caught a whiff of his cologne and sat back down, deciding to leave it open to air out his awful scent.

After another hour, Gwendolyn realized that she had been thrown off by Mr. Trent's visit. As a result, she took just enough time to organize and gather up her papers to store in the safe behind her desk.

She used to keep her papers in a locked dresser until she read *The Firm*, after which she utilized a two-cubic-foot safe. The safe held all her plans for marketing products and her sales strategy. Basically, it stored her ideas. Her ideas, she knew, were like gold, to be protected. If she was the one who thought them up, why wouldn't she treasure them?

Many people do not value their ideas and fret when nobody else does either. If you know what you know, Gwendolyn believed, and you come up with something consisting thereof, then nobody should be able to tell you differently.

She grabbed her purse, looked around her office to be sure she hadn't forgotten anything, then left, closing the door behind her.

As she walked to the elevator to exit the building, she heard her name called by the most annoying voice/person in her world.

"Gwen—Ms. Thompson. I forgot the real reason I came by your office," he said, slinking up to her from whichever toilet he'd crawled out from under.

To harass me mentally and sexually, she thought.

"The boss is coming by tomorrow," he informed her.

The boss? The boss was an alien to her. She never imagined seeing the boss here in the sales and marketing department.

Mr. Quincy, the CEO of Armedia, comes through from time to time to show his face and put on like he were the one making the money flow. He was as bad as Mr. Trent on robbing the credit.

But the controlling stockholder and chairman of Armedia, Inc., coming here was something extraordinary.

"Whoa," was all she could muster in response.

"Yes, whoa," Mr. Trent agreed. "So, we must mind all our Ps and Qs and look alive.

"Ps and Qs. Look alive." What, he thinks we're army cadets? Asshole, she thought but simply nodded her agreement.

"So, chop-chop," he said with two claps. "See you tomorrow," he said, once again trying to make himself uppity-like, but to her, he was just an uptight wannabe.

*   *   *

Octave Royal was an heir/businessman who wanted desperately to make his bones in Corporate America to prove the naysayers and jealous haters wrong. They felt his inheritance and wealthy upbringing were what made him a success. In fact, they did not think he was a success at all, but thought he was just blessed.

Octave knew better, though. His grandfather and his namesake, Octave M. Royal, was a hard worker, and his father, Eugene Royal, was hardly a worker but more so a fuck-up. As a result, Octave's grandfather rarely supported his father's family, which included Octave, his mom Gloria, and brother Julien. It was by Octave's own efforts that he got himself through college at Howard University, then Columbia Business School for his master's. With all said and done, he deserved what he had inherited. No, *he earned* it.

Octave did not earn his inheritance from his education alone, but from his grandfather's tests. Octave Royal the First was an old-fashioned, God-fearing man who was raised with Booker T. Washington's pull-yourself-up-by-the-bootstraps mentality, which meant (1) you earn your keep, and (2) you work for what you want in order not to have to beg or rely on someone else to do for you what you could do yourself. A debt-free concept it was.

Before Octave's grandfather died, he made his lawyer draw out a fine print in his will. He put in a stipulation that no one would inherit his money or business unless they knew the business and how it was that he made his money.

Octave didn't know his grandfather's business, but he knew business in general. It was nothing for him to go online, log in to public records, and research his grandfather's company. He even googled his grandfather and read numerous newspaper and magazine articles that were autobiographic and in chronological order about how the elder Octave built his company. He had started off collecting used bottles and selling them for reuse to beverage companies, which eventually led to inking his first multimillion-dollar deal and later acquiring a media conglomerate.

With this knowledge, the grandson was able to meet his grandfather's expectation and became chairman of his grandfather's company. Although he had done his research, it wasn't until he got the sales and marketing records that really familiarized himself with how the company made money. His grandpa's company wasn't just a media outlet, it was a product-for-sale company.

He obtained the past ten years of sales records and studied the numbers, the presentation and marketing strategies incorporated to sale the products, and really got an idea of what was what. He noted that the growth in sales were mostly within the past five years, when a Mr. Frazier Trent headed the sales and marketing department.

After two and half years of inheriting Armedia, he had never taken it upon himself to visit the sales and marketing department, which had been the key that got him through the door where he sat now. He felt obliged to pay homage to and promote Mr. Trent.

In the office suite of the main executive building for Armedia, Inc., seated behind his desk, Octave leaned back in his chair, scanning through his BlackBerry to see if he had anything else scheduled for the next day besides visiting sales and marketing. He saw that he had an appointment to meet with the current CEO, Mr. Ian Quincy, on company matters. This meeting's agenda would depend on how things went at sales and marketing tomorrow.

He nodded absentmindedly and put his BlackBerry back in the pouch at his waist next to his iPhone. He looked around his office, not believing he was here. Here—the head of a multibillion-dollar corporation. He believed it, yes, but the struggle had been so intense, he felt it surreal when he finally made it. He had started from the bottom, and now he was here. He fought the impulse to jump out of his seat and do an improvised dance, singing the hook of Drake's song that stated the same. He settled for a triumphant smile, although he envisioned himself singing and dancing .

The life of a boss was sweet. He had no worries. But would that always be the case? Murphy's Law said something else, and by its principle, something was bound to happen. He just hoped that when it did, he was able to handle it.

In truth, he was hoping for nothing to happen, and tomorrow was an attempt to establish stability in his company, to prevent anything that would endanger his position on top of the world.

But what he did not know was that having a stable business was nothing in comparison to having a stable life. He was more concerned with stabilizing his company business than his personal business. Not minding the latter could destabilize the former.

Octave bent over to the phone on his desk and pressed a button. "Silvia," he said.

"Yes, sir?" His personal secretary replied.

"Notify my driver. I'm taking it in, and you should do the same," he said.

"All right, Mr. Royal. I will," she said. "Good night."

"Good night," he said, then he looked at his watch to see it was a quarter past five. He usually took it in at six and worked in his home office until eight before calling it a day. But tomorrow was a big day for the future of his enterprise, and he wanted to be well rested.

He got up and left his office. Silvia would take care of organizing his documents before she left, if she had not already seen to it. Not to mention the assortment of clearance to be signed. And she would lock it all up for him.

Silvia was a boss in her own right. Her pay was in the six-figure bracket. Someone ill-informed might think a secretary merely types up letters, keeps up with scheduled appointments, and takes calls—the stereotypical job description of a secretary. However, a secretarial position in a leader's team was a prominent position. She was a key player in the endeavors of the leader and the guiding force behind his momentum.

A leader in her own right is what a secretary is. Plenty of women taking on the secretarial role have utilized their experience and started their own businesses that were even more prosperous than their last employment. Or they have invested in their companies to the point that the 401K retirement plan was certified pocket change. A woman's role in life is a progressive movement.

Chapter 2

Ancient—but not Isis's Ancient—Egypt

Jarmillah Ashanti arrived in Egypt. She stood at its gates, appraising the monumental architecture. The pyramids, obelisks, and the ultimate Sphinx, the lioness. She smiled to herself. She had made it.

Turning her head from side to side, taking in the scene like a surveillance camera, she stood with arms akimbo, inadvertently flexing her muscles. Her physique was one of muscular femininity. Her back and shoulder muscles and biceps protruded, and her legs looked like they belonged to a stallion.

Her dark complexion shone bright under the desert sun. She looked like an athlete-goddess with a prominent nose and full lips. But Jarmillah's eyes were hard. She peered at the world with the gaze of a cobra.

And standing erect, her regal pose was like a king cobra ready to strike. She wore a lion-skin top crisscrossed by straps that held her dagger, poison-tipped darts, and small, round marble rocks with the flute that was used to blow them out, turning them from art to arsenal. She also wore a skirt, accompanied by a sheath that held a sword.

Jarmillah was from the Ashanti tribe of the West African coast. The tribe was famous for its warrior queens. And as any warrior of ancient times was prone to do, Jarmillah traveled the continent looking for new challenges and adventures. Egypt was her last destination before she headed home. She was sure to find a worthy opponent in the land of the gods. Still taking in the sights, she headed to the marketplace.

She wore a small money bag on her hip containing copper, gold, and diamonds as negotiables. She was hungry and thirsty from her journey. The Egyptian marketplace was crowded with buyers and filled with vendors. The travelers weaved about the market, talking and laughing. The chatter in the native tongue was rapid; it sounded annoying to Jarmillah, like morning birds chirping and screeching.

The vendors touted their products for sale: silks of all variety, chalices, gris-gris for sorcery, as well as a variety of cheap souvenirs that hundreds of years later would cause pillagers to kill one another for their value.

Sorcery was a common practice in Egypt. As a matter of fact, Egypt is the birthplace of all the preternatural beings and served as an institution of mystical learning. Prophecy, necromancy, telepathy, and even levitation was taught in Egypt.

Those who excelled in these dark arts would become gods. Many reached this level by a simple show of prudence. The wisest of the time were observers and well disciplined. There were those who knew better, but would not *do* better, and those who were willing to, would not. But when someone, possessing the necessary discipline, knew better and *did* better, she or he became god.

Jarmillah walked through the sea of people, ignoring all the vendors yelling out to her and thrashing their wares in her direction as she passed by. She was not interested in anything that would not fill her stomach.

Her chiseled abs were well defined underneath the leather straps. Her stomach was flat normally, but in her hungry state, it was even flatter. And if the marketplace had not been drowned with the constant birdlike chatter, the masses would have heard her stomach growling. And if they had heard the growl coming from such a small stomach, these superstitious, easily frightened people would have assumed she was possessed by a demon or holding a pygmy captive in her belly.

From one corner of the marketplace, which seemed like the mouth of a river flowing with people, there was a vendor with succulent fruits for sale. Dates, pomegranates, and grapes—not exactly the lion meat she preferred, but her mouth was watering all the same. She pointed to a batch of grapes and dates, then held up three fingers and pointed to the pomegranates.

Jarmillah sat in the shadow on a stone obelisk that was aligned with the Sphinx. The Sphinx was the warrior queen's symbol of prowess. Jarmillah stuffed her face with the luscious fruit, washing it down with a basin filled with mineral water from the Nile River, which she had bought off a traveler when suddenly there had been a stampede of people running away. If their earlier chatter compared to chirping birds, their running was like a flock of birds fleeing from hunters.

Still chewing on a big bite of pomegranate, Jarmillah lifted her head to assess the crowd. She noted the fear on their faces. Instinctively, she dropped her fruits and basin and placed her hand on the hilt of her sword, preparing to draw it at the first sign of danger. She hated fear. It angered her to see the fear scrawled on the people's faces. Fear to the warrior queen was to be confronted and conquered with aggression. Fear was only imagined anyway.

Why fear, Jarmillah thought, something you have not faced but assumed. No one fears wind because they do not see it. They feel wind daily, the most prominent element of the earth, and they dismiss it as   harmless. But when windstorms hit that are capable of moving chariots and camels at the same time, they become fearful of the wind and totally conscious of it. And yet, the wind is capable of disaster every day, at any given time. Therefore, to fear something unseen was as ridiculous as everyday wind to her. Until it blew her away, she did not see it.

A scraggy Egyptian merchant came running past her. She reached out and grabbed him by his bony shoulders.

"What's happening?" she asked in Swahili, the universal language in Africa.

Mumbo jumbo poured out of his mouth. She shook him, firm hands crushing his shoulders.

"Alexander is coming," he finally said.

Her head cocked back like a duck's. Alexander, the Macedonian king, was conquering all types of countries and territories in the known world. Jarmillah had heard of the king and his mighty army outside a village in central Africa.

Now he was coming to try to conquer Egypt. She could feel the excitement boiling in the pit of her stomach. As a warrior, it was the ultimate challenge to fight a worthy opponent. To be the best, or known best, was to become the best. To her, the opportunity to fight a mighty army as great as Alexander's was too good to be true.

She let the man go with a shove, disgusted by the pathetic fear of the unknown he displayed. He could run out of fear of death or great bodily harm, but it was death and harm to live in fear, she thought. Jarmillah shook her head, dismissing the fool, and set off toward the pyramid palace.

*   *   *

The reigning pharaoh was in a frenzy. The blatant disrespect of the young king marching on his kingdom was infuriating. He was yelling and turning blue-black from anger.

"MAN, THE PERIMETER!" he shouted. "CALL UPON EVERY ABLE-BODIED MAN! THE NERVE OF THE ACCURSED DUNGS!"

The orders and rants continued. The court men in the customary skirt and gold straps ran rampant to fulfill the pharaoh's orders, some stopping to obligingly agree to his highness's insults.

One of the courtiers stepped to him amid the chaos. "Sire?" he said.

Pharaoh was in no mood to be distracted from his rants but, hoping for some good news, stopped to address the timid man. "What is it?"

"There's a warrior who requests the privilege to fight in your army," he said.

The privilege to fight in my army, he thought. This must be one of those headstrong young Egyptians who is clearly ignorant of the danger he faces, yet too young to care."

"Is that so?" he asked, voice filled with pride. "Well, have him come forward to receive my blessing."

"*Her*, sire," the courtier said.

Pharaoh didn't register the clarification at first, then it hit him. "'Her'?" he asked, incredulous.

"Yes, I am a woman," Jarmillah answered, approaching the pharaoh in his ruling chamber uninvited. Pharaoh's guards did not stop her from entering. They were too occupied with the imminent war, and not only that. Jarmillah's queenly posture exuded the confidence of a capable, competent fighter that they did not wish to test.

Pharaoh took in Jarmillah's appearance and knew right away that she was the legendary Ashanti, who was said to have fought more battles than any warrior. She was fated to become the next ruler of the tribe but chose to wander around, looking for fights and challenges instead. In all actuality, she was no different from her warrior peers—but she was a woman.

"Who are you?" he asked.

Standing tall, she breathed in, tucking her stomach and raising her chest. She had healthy breasts, and her cleavage, even with the muscles outlined, looked scrumptious—two of the most finely cut black diamonds Pharaoh had ever seen. Jarmillah's muscular structure was solid, but her skin was nothing but soft and delicate.

"I am Ashanti Jarmillah," she declared. "And I wish to, with your blessing, fight in your army against Alexander, sire."

He nodded, wearing a pensive expression. He had no qualms with allowing a woman to fight in his army, especially one as capable as Jarmillah. He wished that the women in his kingdom were more like the Ashanti women. He was going to need all the help he could get. Because if the rumor was true, Alexander's army had multiplied, thanks to the generosity and diplomacy he'd demonstrated to the people of the countries he'd conquered. Alexander made them willing to bear arms and fight for their new king.

"Very well," Pharaoh said. "You have my blessing."

Too excited to speak, Jarmillah nodded and turned on her heels, swishing out to prepare for battle. Pharaoh watched her leave, admiring the way her hips swayed like the wise serpents and the huntress lioness. Surely like the Sphinx, Jarmillah was an extraordinary woman.

Chapter 3

The battle began that evening. Alexander did not waste any time. Upon his arrival, he ordered the trumpets blown to announce their entry. Both armies met in the desert surrounding Pharaoh's kingdom. From a hawk's-eye view it would look like thousands of warriors and hundreds of chariots lined up on both side, the armies' flags flaring like flames.

Alexander sat atop his legendary black horse, restless in her feminine hostility. This was the first omen to Alexander's future success as king and conqueror. He was eager to conquer again.

Jarmillah wore the Ashanti war makeup. Red paint scrolled across both cheeks in a blush. Black ink outlined her eyes, blended with a touch of red to make a reddish-purple color. Her lips were painted with a purple glaze that accentuated her rich chocolate complexion.

In modern times, she might look ready to go on a date with a love interest, rather than prepared for battle. In either time, she was made up to kill.

In ancient Africa, where it originated, makeup was essential to beauty. It represented who a person was, as well as the occasion. Whereas, today, makeup has an association with insecurity—as though a made-up woman is hiding instead of declaring her beauty. If a woman chooses to wear makeup at an opportune time to reflect herself, then it should be taken as an affirming statement. When well applied, makeup and good grooming make it so that men cannot withstand the attraction.

Negativity about makeup is derived from negative minds, and makeup has been the positive representation of a subject since ancient times.

And so made up for her part, Jarmillah held her sword in one hand and a dagger in the other. She was offered a shield, but she declined. Wielding a shield thwarted one's performance on the battlefield, she came to realize;

it caused the warrior to rely on the safety and protection of the shield instead of her offensive skill.

Jarmillah would rather face death and fight to prevent a fatal blow than to rely on a shield for protection. She'd rather be forced to fight like her life depended on it, and in her case it did.

Alexander raised his left arm, and the trumpets blared again, as his left infantry strode out to battle, bellowing their war cry of "Victory!" in at least twenty languages. They were followed by the chariots.

Jarmillah, caring less for dramatics and more anxious to fight, ran toward the throng of warriors headed in her direction.

"EEEEIELL!" she screeched. Running full speed but pacing herself, Jarmillah pointed her sword and dagger out as she fanned her arms to gain momentum. The Egyptian army from all lines launched into battle after her, none wishing to be perceived as any less of a warrior. Jarmillah's sex was nowhere in the equation in their motive to enter battle; no warrior at the time wanted to be outdone by another.

Alexander had no choice but to send his whole frontline in. The battle began. Swords, spears, and scythes swung, and blood splattered, stinging like ammunition from a pellet gun. Blood drenched many of the conquering warriors.

Jarmillah was covered in blood—but not her own—as she stabbed, feinted, and sliced when her opponent fell for the okey-doke. Three to five soldiers rushed her at once, and she took them down, injuring some and killing others.

Her strategy was nothing extraordinary. The warriors were at a disadvantage because they had to face her one by one. If they had managed to surround her on all sides, at the rate they were attacking, they would have defeated her. She may have been able to guard her flank, but an all-around attack would have killed her.

After fifteen minutes of bloodshed and morale dissipating, Alexander raised his balled fist, then released his index and pinky fingers in the sign of the bull. When he did, trumpets blared, and the earth rattled and shook. Everyone halted mid-battle. Alexander's warriors, aware of what was amiss, recovered and scattered. The Egyptians gave chase.

Jarmillah twisted her dagger in a dying warrior, pulled it out, and squinted. In the distance, she saw a cloud of sand. A what-the-fuck expression came over her face. *What devil's magic is this?* she thought. She had encountered sorcery in battle before, but this earth-altering spell was one she was not used to.

Out of the sand cloud came more trumpets blaring and the rumbling of what seemed like an army of giants. It was a herd of elephants.

"Dung!" Jarmillah exclaimed and hurried to take cover. Before she could gain momentum in her stride, a mutant-looking warrior lying on the ground with fatal injuries grabbed her by the ankle, causing her to tumble. She dropped her sword and dagger to catch herself from falling. Jarmillah slid, the skin tearing off her shins. She quickly recovered, scooping herself up on her hands and knees like an animal. The elephants were gaining on her.

She frantically searched for her weapons, hoping to at least recover her sword. No sword, no dagger. She jumped up and looked toward the ugly dying warrior, who gave her a rotten-toothed smile. When his eyes focused behind her, she turned around to see the stampede closing in.

Fuck was her expression. "Fuck" is what she said. She had the impulse to kick the ugly motherfucker in the mouth, but since he was closer to the elephants, she considered it a grave risk.

"Fuck," she said again and dashed out, this time taking account of the men on the ground as she ran.

Just as an elephant was about three steps from trampling her, she dove, knocking herself unconscious.

Jarmillah woke to voices, but she did not open her eyes. She wanted first to listen to ascertain if she was in danger or not. As she listened, she took inventory of her body parts and functions. She felt numb at her wrist and ankles, and her head was throbbing. She stole a peek and only saw a darkened sky and the flames from torches in the distance. She tried to move but found herself unable to.

She realized she was tied up on the ground by her wrists and ankles, her arms and legs spread out. She was captured. But how? All she could recall was diving out of the elephant's way. She lifted her head and an agonizing pain hit her like a sledgehammer.

"Ahh", she moaned and cursed herself for doing so. It was sure to garner attention. There was almost no other noise in this desert.

"She wakes," she heard someone say, as she lowered her head to compose herself.

She heard a group of people coming toward her. She slowly raised her head again to face her captors—to fix their faces to fix in mind in case they were stupid enough to let her go alive. They were warriors of Alexander's army, men of diverse races and cultures. Jarmillah looked at each with cold, defiant eyes, vying for revenge.

She guessed that when she took her dive, her head hit a stone. She was captured while she was unconscious. What she did not know was that the elephants trampled a quarter of Pharaoh's army and Alexander's army took advantage of the element of surprise. They ended up routing Pharaoh's army, capturing some but almost killing them all.

Alexander had every intent on conquering the age-old, legendary land. The birthplace of gods. And believing his mother, who told him that he was the son of a god, he knew he was destined to rule such a place.

The men stood around Jarmillah, making fun of how weak the Egyptian army was that they needed a woman to fight for them. They spoke in a foreign tongue that was not Aramaic, nor Swahili, nor Arabic. Nonetheless, she was able to understand because she had traveled extensively to many of the surrounding countries since leaving the Ashanti.

"Why don't you untie me then?" she quipped, "since you all are so big and bad."

They laughed, but their mirth was only on the surface because they knew the warrior queen was not one to mess with. Jarmillah rolled her eyes, knowing they knew better. Then the laughter ceased; in fact, no sound was heard at all, except for the distinctive huffs and footsteps of an approaching horse.

Jarmillah looked up to see a jet-black stallion carrying a sunburnt white man with flowing blonde hair and a beak-like nose. It was Alexander, she knew, not only from the reverent silence his arrival caused, but from the intense glare of his yellow-hazel eyes. It was a look that radiated confidence—a look that said, "I am the shit around here."

She returned his gaze with one of confident defiance. Her look said, "I'll kill you as soon as I get the chance." Alexander peered into her chocolate-brown eyes and read their hostile message. Then he traced her body with his eyes, from her face down to her structured breasts, to her chiseled abs—all the way down her sculpted, thick thighs to her feet, then back to her face. When he looked back in her eyes, his expression had changed from strength to lust.

He dismounted his horse, and one of his men grabbed the reins. All the while, Alexander kept his lustful gaze fastened on her.

It was readily seen that he was taken by Jarmillah. Her strength and physique were attractive. Alexander, although gay, was turned on by her strength, resolve, and tenacity. An independent woman. A woman who had her own mind, who thought for herself and who was determined to live by her own means. And her soft skin covering such hard muscles turned Alexander on.

The silent strength of this woman aroused the king. She was like his mother, who inculcated in him since birth his greatness. A woman of this intelligence was a true queen who defied the subjugation that was expected of a woman.

However, a woman of such defiance was rare. As a result, Alexander had taken notice of men who were masculine, yet they donned robes, long and short, and grew long, flowing hair. The young king associated masculinity with the intelligence and independence of a woman. A woman with such strength appealed to Alexander, who had an incestuous love for his mother, but he had met no such woman at home or throughout the countries he had conquered. Until now.

Prior to this encounter, he had inquired about Jarmillah. He had become excited from what he found out about the warrior queen from the Ashanti tribe. Her conquest and tenacity. She was the woman of his dreams, but he knew she would not be his—at least not by her choice.

Jarmillah eyed the king, recognizing his attraction to her. She knew what was to come of her captivity. Raping and pillaging were synonymous with war. Alexander disrobed right there, standing before her in his pale bronze and pink glory. He already had an erection, revealing to the queen that it was his metal sword that was more dangerous than his man sword. The latter would not be doing any kind of serious stabbing.

Tied up on the ground, legs already spread and her skirt giving no cover, Jarmillah was vulnerable. Alexander mounted her. He made the mistake of leaning his face down to hers, enabling the queen to take a bite at his neck, attempting to rip out his jugular, but the king tore away from her in the nick of time.

"DUNG!" he cried. His men instinctively came forward. "Sack up!" he commanded, and they stopped in their tracks. As the pain from Jarmillah's bite subsided, Alexander was even more turned on.

He remained up in a pushup position as he penetrated her. To his surprise and pleasure, she lifted her hips and thrust herself at him. Their bodies met in a clapping sequence. He looked down at her, expecting to see, to his manly pride, a look of satisfaction on Jarmillah's face. Instead, he saw a look of angry determination—a look that said, "I am the one raping you."

This too turned the king on. He felt himself about to ejaculate. She must have felt it, too, because she sped up her thrusts. Jarmillah was determined to rape the legendary king—to conquer the conqueror.

She worked her hips, which expedited an ejaculation. The king came inside of her, then quickly ordered his men to pull him off of her. From the climax he'd just had, he was bound to drop on top of her, defenseless to the warrior queen's sure strike.

Jarmillah smirked as they pulled Alexander off. Embarrassed, but sexually satisfied, he said, "Release her, and banish her far from me."

He grabbed his robe off the ground and put it on. His face was red, and sweat fell from his forehead.

He turned on all his men. "And none of you shall speak of this again"— the night that Alexander the Great was raped by an African Queen.

Chapter 4

Modern-day Miami, Florida

Gwendolyn showed up to work at 6:00 a.m., as normal, beating the early rush-hour traffic. As her coworkers arrived, also early, she noticed the tension in the office. This, she knew, could be attributed to Mr. Trent's poor management skills, but also to the imminent arrival of the chairman of the board and boss of Armedia. The visit would cause Mr. Trent to heighten the pressure in the sales and marketing department, making everyone uncomfortable.

She wasn't the least bit surprised to see Mr. Trent barging into her office before she could even turn on her computer.

"Gwen." She fixed him with a stern stare. "Ms. Thompson," he corrected himself, "where is the summary of the quarter's performance?"

"Where it always is," she said. She refused to allow him to rattle her up like he did the rest of the department. He stood still for a moment. Gwendolyn thought he was dumbstruck—struck by how dumb he was.

He scratched his head—a gesture common to a wild monkey, which did not make any sense and made it *look* like it had no sense.

"O—okay then," he stammered. "Well." With the hand that wasn't scratching his head, he began fiddling with his vest button, completing the dumb monkey image.

"Are you ready?" he finally asked.

"Yes, sir," she replied with a too-big smile. She was tickled by his monkey business.

"Very well then," he said. After he left, she burst out laughing and shaking her head.

* * *

Octave was anxious to meet Mr. Trent. He was intending to compensate the head of sales and marketing. If it were not for Mr. Trent's memo reporting the quarter summaries of Armedia's sales performance, Octave would not be where he was today.

Chauffeured in his SUV Porsche Cayenne, he peered out the window at the Armedia, Inc., office building. Once again, he was hit with the realization of where he had landed. The SUV pulled into the executive parking lot next to the private elevator. He looked at his watch and saw that the shiny gold arrows pointed to 7:00 a.m.

His meeting was for 7:15, and he liked to be either punctual or early. He was an efficient man, about his business. He was ready to change the course of Armedia, Inc.—to take it to the next level. The Internet of things (IOT) movement in technology was dominating. He planned to steer the company toward developing and selling such devices and conveniences. Their stock was sure to rise, placing his company in the league with Apple and Microsoft.

*   *   *

Mr. Trent was delegating—or dictating—to his secretary to display a variety of pastries and beverages in case the chairman wanted breakfast when he arrived.

There was no one at the secretary's desk, so Octave let himself in.

"Hurry, Gloria," Mr. Trent said, annoyed. "It's after seven o'clock already. You'd think I wouldn't have to tell you this."

"Yes, sir," she said, thinking, *You didn't. You're just an ass kisser who likes to fatten the stomach up to eat the shit as well.*

"Dammit!" Mr. Trent exclaimed, looking at his watch.

Octave took in the scene and thought Mr. Trent was being a little too harsh.

Gloria seemed unperturbed, though, which told him that she was confident in her ability to handle her business, and Mr. Trent's rudeness was uncalled for. But this was his opinion; he might be wrong.

Octave decided to make his presence known. "Ahem," he cleared his throat. Gloria and Mr. Trent stopped in their tracks—well, Gloria stopped in her tracks while Mr. Trent stopped mid-blabber.

"Mr. Royal," Mr. Trent said, recovering from his shock and hoping he was not being judged for his behavior toward his secretary. "A pleasure to see you, sir."

May I start kissing yo ass? Gloria thought, finishing Mr. Trent's ass-kissing greeting. She smiled at Mr. Royal and gave him a polite nod.

To her surprise, Octave said, "Good morning—um, Gloria. If I may?"

"Yes, sir," she said. "I prefer you do." She caught in her peripheral vision Mr. Trent cutting his eyes at her. He probably felt that he was not the only one who knew how to kiss ass. But the difference was that Gloria was being acknowledged without going out of her way and was courteous in response.

"Thank you. It's an honor," he said warmly. "I am—"

"Sir, I know who you are," she cut him off. "And it's a pleasure meeting you."

"All right, Gloria, you may leave us," Mr. Trent quipped, wanting to push his secretary out of the way to be the only ass-kisser.

"Okay," she said, embarrassed by his rude dismissal. Octave noted her discomfort.

"Gloria, may I have one of those delicious-looking pastries? The doughnut with the crust, please?"

"Yes, sir," she said, feeling appreciated. "Would you like something to drink?"

"Orange juice, please."

While Gloria busied herself with the refreshments, Octave turned to Mr. Trent with a serious expression. "Do you have the quarter summary?" He had some misgivings about Mr. Trent. The vibes he was getting from him felt bad. However, he decided to put personal feelings aside and get down to business. It was Mr. Trent's business acumen he was interested in anyway.

"I'm expecting a general copy," he began but cut himself off, remembering Ms. Thompson said it was waiting in the usual place. "Actually, I have it here."

He walked to his drop box and retrieved the documents. Octave wondered why he had to have a general copy, but it sounded efficient.

Mr. Trent opened the folder. "Well, we generated sales of ten million dollars on commercial advertisement and—"

"Let me see it for myself," Octave interjected. Mr. Trent passed the papers to him. Octave walked to one of the two chairs at Mr. Trent's mahogany desk and sat down. Gloria sat the doughnut on a napkin on the desk and a Styrofoam cup filled with orange juice next to it.

Octave opened the folder, looked up at her, and said, "Thank you, Gloria."

"You're welcome," she said, feeling more pleased because she knew Mr. Royal would remember her by name. A simple consideration that was the highest compliment in her field. It was not often that an executive, especially one as high in the ranks as Mr. Royal, remembered a secretary's name. She scurried out of the office, wearing what would appear to be a permanent smile.

Octave turned his attention to the documents, scanning past the hyperbole and straight to the numbers. He came to the devices' sales records and liked what he saw. The sales of electronic devices were up to the roof—sixty million this quarter alone. He felt himself get excited. It's one thing to have an idea about something but another to find out you were on point.

Mr. Trent, noticing the look of pleasure on Octave's face, said, "Yes, it's something," but not knowing what it was since he had yet to read the quarterly summary report himself.

"Indeed, it is," Octave agreed. "This coincides with my vision for our company."

Mr. Trent nodded, not sure what to say in response. He wasn't a company man; he was his own man, in it for himself.

"This is beautiful," Octave said. "Do you have the prediction for future project earnings?"

"Sure," Mr. Trent said, then he stepped around his desk and pressed a button on the phone. It rang twice before it made a loud clicking sound to indicate the call answered.

"Gloria, get Ms. Thompson and have her meet me in my office." Then he clicked the button to hang up.

He didn't bother to say "please." Octave was beginning to feel disturbed by Mr. Trent's mannerisms, but once again he held his personal views to himself.

"Who is Ms. Thompson?" he asked.

"She's one of my leading team members, whom I have trained personally," he said, taking the credit for Gwendolyn's work, knowing she was the best at what she did.

"Well, let's go see her," Octave said.

*   *   *

"What is in the core of an apple?" Gwendolyn asked herself. She was seated with a notepad on her desk and a pen in hand, tapping it to her chin.

An apple has been the most commonly consumed fruit since the beginning of time. The apple has so many connotations that Gwendolyn considered it an ideal marketing resource, or a thought-provoking fruit.

She was contemplating a marketing strategy to promote the sale of a canister with electronic capabilities to keep warm or cool and alert its owners of the contents inside. It was for the science industry. With this canister, scientists could take their research to another level, concerning certain bio substances that needed preservation to perform the necessary tests to complete theories.

A groundbreaking device, she thought. *Groundbreaking....*

At the core of an apple is its seeds, she ruminated. *And for seeds to produce, they must be planted, then watered, for them to grow.* So with this in mind, she thought, if she "planted" the canister in the right "soil," where she thought potential consumers would be, and then broadcast advertisements, or "watered" it in other words, the device would "grow" in sales.

She smiled and scribbled all this down on her notepad. *Finished.* She rose, peering down on her written idea with a satisfied smile.

"I did that," she boasted, as Mr. Trent and Octave entered her office. Mr. Trent knocked on her door as he opened it, basically intruding. She needed to get a lock. *Wait a minute*—she did have a lock, so he must have opened it with his master key. *The nerve of that bastard.* Smile replaced with a set jaw and stern expression, Gwendolyn glared at him, not noticing his company or, in her anger, merging them together as one.

"What was it that you did?" Mr. Trent asked.

"Work," she answered simply.

He laughed a phony, pompous-ass laugh. "That's funny," he said, turning to Octave. "Mr. Royal, she has a great sense of humor."

Judging by her expression, Octave did not think so. But he knew Mr. Trent was trying to lighten the situation and capture her attention.

Gwendolyn caught on quickly. Not wanting to seem like a bitch but refusing to accept a violation of her privacy, she said, "Good morning, gentlemen. How can I help you? As I said, I am working." Polite but dismissing.

"I was informing Mr. Royal about our itinerary for projected sales earnings," Mr. Trent said, hoping she would take on the task of introduction.

Gwendolyn sat there staring. She intended to make him sweat because she knew he had his lips puckered, possibly locked on, kissing the boss of bosses' ass. After an uncomfortable moment, she nodded. No "Okay, sir. Let me get it," or "Yes sir, it is right here. Anything to oblige the boss."

He thought he could just barge into her office and ask her for something. As if by saying "Jump," she would. It was his job as the supervisor of sales and marketing to present this information to the higher-ups and need-to-knows.

So she didn't feel obligated to volunteer this information, especially after the rudeness of this turd.

"Well, can we see it?" he asked. The sarcastic "well" she knew was Mr. Trent asserting his authority, but she would wait for him to beg. She still did not budge.

Octave Royal, already exposed to Mr. Trent's lack of diplomacy and communication skills, thought it would be a good time to implement his own.

"Ms. Thompson," he began, walking up to her desk. "Sorry for barging in on you, but I was eager to see the sales predictions. I'm Mr. Royal, the chairman of Armedia," he said, sticking out his hand.

She took it. An apology was required and acceptable, she felt, but he was no less demanding than Mr. Trent. Perhaps he was even more so, intimidating as he was with his tall and—judging by the way his suit fit him perfectly—muscular physique. Then telling her who he was, like she was supposed to stop what she was doing to please him, giving his own command to jump.

"With all due respect, sir. I am not prepared to present to you what you ask," she said.

"Why not?" he asked.

The nerve, Gwendolyn thought. It seemed the more a man rose in rank, the more self-centered and power hungry he became.

She made a promise to herself to never get that way when she rose in rank. In her book, a rise in professional standing, financial status, or prestige was not a physical level, where you could look down at people, but rather a grounded position to do right by others.

"Because" she began, "it is not a discussion of sports that's filled with gobbledygook. It's a presentation that is economical, as well as psychological. Our overall agenda is to present products to a receptive economy. And economy is people, which is where the psychological standpoint must be analyzed.

"Our key goal is not to target our customers, but to help them help us. And to present such a prediction at a minute's notice would only outline the broader aspect of sales. I am not comfortable with presenting half-ass data," she concluded.

Octave was taken aback. He felt like a child who had been chastised for committing a no-no. He thought he was being considerate, but it was obvious she felt insulted.

Gwendolyn's response impressed him. Hearing her say "our" told him she was a team player, and her meticulous response demonstrated great potential and a hell of an asset to the company. Not to mention a hell of a woman, but he would keep his personal views to himself. The question was, how could he make up for offending her?

"I see," he said, nodding like a bobblehead. "I am sorry. I didn't know." He decided to apologize and to keep that apology short and simple. Colorful words or a long explanation would only serve to make him seem more wrong than remorseful.

When wrong is done, it is unproductive to extend an apology. To do so would be dwelling in it, and the offender would make the offended feel more so. Instead of alleviating the wrong, it escalates it.

She just nodded, acknowledging his apology. He looked into her eyes, hoping to see that his apology was received properly, but he really could not tell. Her facial expression softened, but it was difficult to imagine what she was thinking.

She watched him trying to read her. What made him think she was an open-book type of woman to be read at will? Well, she was not.

"Perhaps you would like to schedule a date to receive the predictions," she said.

"A date?" he asked, raising his eyebrows.

"Yes, a date you would like to review the report or have it emailed to you."

Disappointed by her clarification and mad at himself for assuming more than a professional definition of the word *date*, he said, "Yes, that will be appropriate."

"Which?"

He thought she said *witch*. An appropriate title for her, since he was bewitched by her. His attraction was building by the minute. He stared at her, dumbfounded.

Gwendolyn could tell he didn't understand. *And this is supposed to be the boss of bosses,* she thought. She clarified, "*Which* would you prefer—a personal presentation of the documents or an email?"

"Oh," he said. "Um, email it to me." He did not trust himself in her presence again. There was something about her that did something to him.

She shrugged and murmured, "OK."

"Thank you," he said.

"Well, then, sir," Mr. Trent began. "Let's return to my office and discuss matters."

As a man, Mr. Trent knew that Octave was turned on by Gwendolyn. Her light-brown complexion with the even lighter brown eyes to match and set jaw supporting a pair of luscious lips, accentuated by outliner and lip gloss—she radiated a raw sex appeal. The type of woman who appeals to a man without being provocative. Only a few women possess this type of attraction.

Hers was a power and sway over the male species. Her body was not the typical hourglass shape or thickness that caught the attention of most men, though. Gwendolyn had a pear shape that was as succulent as her lips. Like Phylicia Rashad or a vintage wine, she possessed a lasting beauty that would only get finer with time.

"Carry on, Ms. Thompson," Mr. Trent said. Then to Octave, "Shall we, sir?"

"Yes," Octave said. "Good day, ma'am."

He considered shaking her hand but thought against it. He did not want to have his handshake linger. She seemed to possess an energy that could charge a man. Or did he crave to feel her touch?

Octave turned to leave, fighting the urge to look back. He walked out with Mr. Trent in tow. Gwendolyn watched them leave, and when they did, she went right back to work.

Chapter 5

Octave was back at his office, seated behind his iron desk, and contemplating his plan to take the company to the next level. After meeting Mr. Trent, he had misgivings about awarding him the CEO spot. The man was clearly a dick. His poor communication skills were a sure future snag in the movement of the company. Octave needed productive people in place to see his plan come to fruition, and neither Mr. Trent nor Mr. Quincy, the current CEO, were fit for the team he was formulating.

Nevertheless, he had to make do with what he had or else take on the operation himself. That was not a bad idea. Even Bill Gates once wore the titles of chairman and CEO. Octave leaned back in his chair. He had to seriously consider that move—a move he knew was appropriate but not necessary. It was his vision he wanted to see through, and he had the passion that was required. Therefore, he was more than suitable for the job. And this was a venture, he knew, that was a chance to build his legacy as his grandfather before him did.

As he imagined himself handling the day to day and delegating to his team to bring to life the picture of the company he had envisioned, the phone on his desk rang. He raised up the receiver and pressed a button on the phone. "Yes?"

"Sir," Silvia, his secretary, said, "your brother's here."

Brother? What did his brother want? "All right, Silvia. Send him in, please," he said. The only way to find out what his brother wanted was to ask him outright.

His brother entered his office, which was the size of a typical apartment.

Octave stood up. "Julien, how have you been?"

Julien Royal did not speak but walked toward his brother. Octave took him in. He wore a suit and carried a briefcase—a rarity for his little brother, who was younger only by a minute and eighteen seconds. He was more of a jeans-and-jacket type. A B-boy style. The corporate fashion looked odd on him.

Julien stopped in front of the desk and placed his briefcase on top. "Octave, I have come to stake my claim in the family business," he said.

Octave leaned his head back and forth, duck-like, not understanding what his brother was saying.

"I'm a shareholder of nearly thirty percent of the stock," Julien continued, "which makes me a key board member with the leeway to partake in the business." This was true, but Octave had never known Julien to be interested in the business at all. He was more into partying and bullshitting.

"What gave you the change of heart?"

Julien smirked. "Money!"

Of course, money was the motive; however, Julien was well endowed. Octave made sure of that. He had at least twenty million dollars in assets and a good portion of actual money to boot.

But what Octave did not know was that Julien wanted to run the company as bad as he did because he wanted to run it as bad as he could. He was tired of his brother trying to outdo him. Then bird-feeding him with the little bit of millions when the company was worth billions of dollars. That, Julien felt, was an insult.

"But you're not hurting for money," Octave told him.

"With the peanuts I have currently," he sucked his teeth, "that will not always be the case."

His brother's spending habits and carefree attitude flashed in Octave's mind, which made what Julien said ring true. And with Julien's habits in mind, Octave knew that the future of the company was at risk. No way he would allow his brother to destroy the business.

Octave shook his head. "Have you giving this some real thought, Julien?" he asked patiently. Maybe this was just a phase he was going through.

"There is not such a thing as a fake thought, Octie," he replied, intending to strike a nerve in his brother, who hated that nickname. Octave ground his teeth, refusing to let his emotions get involved.

This was a serious matter that could affect his life's goal. He decided to go another route. "Julien, what role you wish to play in the company?" he asked.

"I thought CEO would be suitable for me."

"CEO!" Octave exclaimed, all calm flying out the door. "What makes you think you can take on such a role?"

"I am a Royal," Julien replied.

"A Royal?" Octave asked, incredulous. "A Royal," he repeated, shaking his head. "Really? Being part of the family doesn't make you qualified. That's nuts."

"Are you finished?" Julien calmly asked. "Because I sure wasn't."

Wearing a frown, as if he were the unstable brother, Octave said, "No, I am not, but I would love to hear more of what you have to say."

"I know you have no faith in my ability to run the company, but I have been studying and taking business management classes to ensure that I get the job done."

"Congratulations. You have shown interest in business, but what makes you think you could run *this* business?"

Julien reached down, opened his briefcase, and pulled out a small stack of papers stapled at the top left corner. He handed them to Octave. "Here you go." Octave took the papers with a frown. "I will be laying my claim to the board in two weeks," Julien informed him. He closed his briefcase, picked it up— official-like—and made his leave, his brother seething.

Octave wanted to slam the papers down on his desk, or better yet, in the trash. But he knew better. He began reading the front page. He had to be prepared to counter his brother's argument for the CEO seat. He might find more reasons to place himself there in the documents.

*   *   *

Gwendolyn finished preparing the presentation at 5:00 p.m. and sent for a courier to mail it out. She was done and ready to go home. The long day was over. She had completed outlining her marketing strategy.

Tomorrow, she knew, would bring other tasks, but at least she wasn't leaving unfinished work behind. That was something she hated to do, and on the rare occasions when she did, she was not herself. It felt as if she were attaching a new effort to an old deed. Like young legs on an old body, it would walk and run fine, but the new parts didn't look quite right. The entire body of work would have parts that performed different functions—some moving accordingly, others barely moving. Therefore, finished work was a balanced body of work that functioned on one accord.

As a ritual, she gathered her papers up and stuffed some in her locker; the important papers she put in the safe.

She arrived at her house at a quarter past seven. The drive to and from work counted as work hours, and she could deduct the gas cost on her income tax. Otherwise, she would be working to lose money.

Her driveway was lit by little lights implanted in the grass lining the pavement. She parked her car, a pink Lexus coupe, and used the electronic key to secure the doors. She stepped onto her front stoop and peered out at her front yard.

The manicured lawn, perfectly trimmed cherry bushes, and expansive landscaping was not what caught her attention. She was reminded of when she was a little girl, living with her beloved late mother, who instilled in her the pull-yourself-up-by-the-bootstraps mentality.

Little Gwendolyn approached her mother in the living room. "Mommy, can I have a My Little Pony doll?" she pleaded.

"If you want it, you will have to buy it yourself. Chile, I am broke," her mother said. This declaration was alien to the eight-year-old little girl. If her mother could not buy it, how on earth was she going to afford it?

Face scrunched in confusion, she asked, "Mommy, how am I gonna if you not gonna?"

"That is something you need to ask yourself," her mother said, walking to the kitchen. Little Gwendolyn followed. She was considering the question as she sat down at the table inside their small kitchen.

Her mother turned and asked, "Sweetie, you want some lemonade?"

Lost in thought, yet hoping her mother would admit she was teasing, absentmindedly said, "Yes, ma'am." Her mother pulled out a jar and sugar from the top cabinets and opened the refrigerator and pulled out a bag of lemons. Then she slightly slammed them all down on the kitchen counter.

Little Gwendolyn looked up at the noise. She saw all the ingredients to make the lemonade and was kind of disappointed. She knew her mother squeezed her own lemonade, but thought they already had some made. Suddenly, she experienced the proverbial "aha moment."

Later that day, after getting her mother's permission, little Gwendolyn threw a clean cloth over an old table in the front yard, on which she sat a jug of lemonade next to a cooler of ice.

Leaned against the table was a cardboard sign, advertising "Ice-Cold Lemonade" for sale. She would not put the ice inside the lemonade pitcher until the customer bought a cup, because the ice was likely to melt and ruin the flavor of the lemonade.

The enterprising little Gwendolyn sat at her lemonade stand when two little boys about her age came by. "Ya'll wanna buy some lemonade?" she asked them.

"No, we wanna take a cup," one of the boys said. This was Roger; she knew him from school, and the other boy was Rick, who she knew from school too.

After Roger stated their objective, Rick took it upon himself to grab one of the plastic cups.

"Put that back if you are not buying," little Gwendolyn protested. The boys laughed. This made her angry. She set her face in the meanest glare she thought her mother would wear, then said, "If you don't cut it out and leave, I'll do…something." That sounded like something her mother would say.

"If we don't, then what?" Roger asked, teasing.

She did not think that far ahead. Then what? she thought. Bust them upside their heads?

She knew she could, but they could jump her. Shoo, she thought. They could beat me up, two against one. So, muscling the boys was out of the question. Then she recalled the way Roger used to stare at her when they were in second grade. She knew he liked her, but young boys had a terrible way of acknowledging a girl. Or they were scared to. She also knew that boys hated to be called out for liking girls. Little Gwendolyn decided to use this tactic.

She tilted her head and looked up at Roger with puppy-dog eyes. "You only messing with me because you like me," she said in the sweetest voice she could muster.

Roger, who had a light brown complexion, turned fire-red. "Nuh-uhn," he denied.

"Yeah, huh," she said, then turned to Rick. "He used to blow me kisses and all." She decided to rub it in deep.

"For real, man?" Rick asked him.

"No, I didn't."

"Yeah, he did." Little Gwendolyn retorted.

"She is lying on me," Roger defended himself.

"Lying about what?"

"That I blew kisses at you."

"But you do like me, though?" she said, fluttering her eyes.

Roger realized that by disclaiming one accusation he served to admit to another. He could not say anything. He just stared at her with a ghastly glare.

Rick, feeling played by his homeboy for using him to try and get to her, said, "Man, I am gone." He threw down the cup and briskly walked away. Rick had a crush on Gwendolyn, too, and feared she might spray him like she did Roger.

"C'mon, man," Roger pleaded. Then he turned to little Gwendolyn, his face scrunched, mean-mugging her.

Little Gwendolyn blew him a kiss, causing his face to redden even more. Knowing she was taunting him, yet feeling helpless because he did kind of like her, Roger stormed off in Rick's trail.

Little Gwendolyn laughed, then shouted, "LEMONADE! GETCHA LEMONADE!" Back to business.

Gwendolyn shook her head and smiled at the memory. She went inside. Suddenly, she was feeling tired, but she knew it was not physical. Constantly battling boys was mentally exhausting. Like her encounter with her bosses. The nerve of them. Mr. Royal was no different than arrogant Mr. Trent. Although he tried to be polite, he only served to offend her even more.

She walked to her bedroom, setting down her purse and kicking off her pumps. She would get them in the morning.

Even though Mr. Royal was attractive, his arrogance was not. He had a dark complexion that was appealing to her. As a light-skinned Black woman, she did not believe she had a preference, like the saying, "Red girls like dark-skinned men" and vice versa. Gwendolyn liked what she liked, and the dark-skinned Mr. Royal she liked. Well, she liked his complexion. Not to mention his shape. Even over his tailored suit she could tell he had a muscular build or at least he was in shape. And his lips—those full, juicy lips. She shook her head.

She did not need thoughts like that right before bed, sparking inappropriate images in dreams that could cause wet discomfort. *Sheesh!* She crashed into bed, and sleep encompassed her immediately.

Chapter 6

Ancient—but not Isis's nor Jarmillah's Ancient—Egypt

Under the starry desert sky, the woman stared in the girl's eyes, seeing a double image of herself. Their big oval, azure eyes were both brightened—one set by the fervent need to inculcate a lesson, and the other from trying her best to show she was paying attention.

The girl, who was sixteen years old, was glad her mother was not holding her by the shoulders in the process.

"Listen to me," the mother said. The girl—*thinking, What the hell I have been doing all along?*—nodded.

The mother and daughter were descendants of Jarmillah. After the warrior queen had raped and humiliated Alexander, she had been released.

Jarmillah had roamed the land for months, challenging warriors and defeating those who were foolish enough to accept her challenge. In her mind, she was still fighting Alexander and his army of mutts. She was as angry as a mad dog about her capture—a capture not by honorable defeat but by a bump on the head. Her anger was mixed with a rollercoaster of emotions. She cried at times, frowned at others, and made smudgy smirks now and again.

Jarmillah could not understand why she was feeling like this. Sometimes she felt all these emotions in an hour without transition. After a few weeks of this and other telltale signs, she realized she was pregnant. Her warrior days were momentarily over. Her strong desire to fight was weakened by a maternal responsibility.

When she delivered her baby, she knew that she would have to instill in her child the warrior's mentality of survival. When her daughter,

Cormelia, was five years old, peering up at her with big saucer eyes that were grayish blue marbled with green, Jarmillah let her know she was a queen.

A queen not only of the Ashanti, but of all Egypt, for she was the descendant of the reigning king, Alexander. For Jarmillah knew it was a man's world, but that it would not turn without a woman.

"Never let yourself be conquered by a man," she told her daughter, and the little girl nodded.

Now centuries later, Cormelia the fourteenth was instilling in her daughter a philosophy of her own. "Sway Rule" she called it. Cormelia knew the male species was dominating in Eastern Africa and abroad. For centuries, the known world had been matriarchal.

Women were either worshipped or honored. The bloodline of a clan had been determined by the women. Now, however, men were on the verge of establishing a patriarchy. They had already destroyed the Sphinx's nose to alter its sex and declared the phallic monument, obelisk, a symbol of the assumed power structure of the male species. But this symbol of male strength was their weakness.

"A man would go to war for a woman," she told her daughter Cleopatra. "He would go to the extreme to protect her.

"When men are boys, they supposedly hate girls. But when they become men, they will do anything to make an impression on a woman. So, it's on the woman to cause this possessiveness in a man."

"How do I do that, my queen?" Cleopatra asked. (It was custom in Africa for children to address their mothers as their queen. She was the ruler of their existence, the pampered and controlling force in their lives until they were old enough to rule on their own.)

"Your sex is a man's most demanding object of desire," she explained. "Diamonds are the most precious rocks that Africa has produced.

Ornaments of beauty, unbreakable rocks that symbolize beauty and wealth.

"Diamonds have been considered a girl's best friend, meaning that they cherish them and would do anything to possess them. But that is a surface interpretation. A diamond, or the shape of a diamond, is a V. A woman's most precious possession—an ornament of the greatest wealth, life, and pleasure. And this pleasure of life is what men cherish. They would kill for and die to possess it. Even when we are not making it available for possession.

"The latter foolish thought is where your power is derived. The carrot on the stick always moves a donkey." Cleopatra nodded, wearing a pensive expression. "Never allow yourself to be conquered by a man. You are a queen. Always know it," Cormelia told her. "When you rule your being, you know a worthy man. But in the ruling of a nation, you rule as the one worthy of that power."

"Yes, my queen," Cleopatra said. Her chest was filled with boiling hot pride. She was proud to be born as the species in possession of a powerful rock. Like the most expensive rock, it shone, deserving to be honored, cherished, and respected. *Women rock!* She felt queenly by her mother's description of a woman alone.

After letting her words take root, Cormelia told Cleopatra, "Now, go claim your throne."

Chapter 7

Two years later

The pharaoh was worried about his bastard offspring, Tuteh. Weeks had past, and there hadn't been any sign of him. Well, there had been sightings of him at night, but nothing during the day.

What Tuteh did during day his father did not understand, nor why he chose to roam the kingdom at night, staying aloof and away from Pharaoh's palace.

He chose to stay away at a time like this, Pharaoh thought. It was Tuteh's twenty-first birthday and the country was at war. The fate of Egypt relied on an able young body to rule and fight with the impetuosity common to youth.

Rome was on the horizon, and like the sun, the empire wanted to burn away any other kingdom in its path. Pharaoh was approaching old age, and the time had come to crown his son and give him his birthright. The god Osiris blessed his greatest of great-grandfathers' lineage, making all his descendants pharaohs, and the namesake of the greatest of great-grandfathers was supposed to claim the throne and rule, preserving the bloodline.

However, when Alexander conquered Egypt, it complicated things. The ruling force was to align and bestow whomever he chose, and a bloodline heir was the next in line for the throne. The latter was not possible because Alexander had no such lineage in Egypt. Therefore, Tuteh would fulfill the god's blessing. But where in hell's fire was Tuteh? Pharaoh was pacing in his throne room when a courtier came to him.

"Sire," he said. Pharaoh stopped mid-pace, cocked his head back from its lowered position, and turned to the courtier, who awaited the pharaoh's permission to speak.

"What is it, Jaffé?" the pharaoh asked.

"There's a young woman who wishes to see you, sire."

A young woman wants to see me? Is it another Helfer wishing to see my royal staff in private? He chuckled at that. "Who is it?" he asked.

"A Cleopatra, sire," Jaffé answered.

"Cleopatra," he repeated, although his tone asked, "Cleopatra who?"

"She says she's come to claim her throne," Jaffé told him.

Claim her throne, he thought, rubbing his chin. Is she another bastard? And what makes her, a female, think she can rule over Egypt? "Tell me, Jaffé, is she fuckable?"

Jaffé didn't know what to say. He did not want to answer such a vulgar question. For one, he didn't want to say something unpleasing to Pharaoh, and for another, he didn't want to say something that may come back and bite him under the new pharaoh if she was the real deal.

"Shall I show her in, sire?" he asked, instead of answering.

"You are a smart man, Jaffé," the pharaoh commended. "Bring the Helfer in then, and let's rest this matter." *Maybe Tuteh's spirit was so restless for a bloodline continuance that it would choose a woman to rule.*

Cleopatra walked into the room in a slow, elegant prance, head bowed subserviently. She floated to the middle of the room, then stopped. Head still bowed.

"Approach, fair servant," Pharaoh said, standing in front of his throne. She commenced to walk toward him and slowly lifted her head to look him in the eyes.

"What—" he gasped. Her eyes were twin rainbows springing from a gray cloud, and her being was the treasure at the end of the rainbows. She was plump for times when slender women were the norm. Her stomach poked out and her thighs were as thick as the Mongols' horses, with a curved, round butt that resembled an enlarged pomegranate.

Pharaoh could not understand her attraction, but she was attractive. The nose that split her beautiful eyes was long, as though perfected by a sculptor.

Cleopatra knew the effect she had on men because she intended it. She took it upon herself to lay her claim, snapping the pharaoh from his trance. "I am Cleopatra, the magnificent," she said in a soft, harmonious tone. Every breath of her words was alluring. "I have come to claim my throne," she declared with the self-assurance of real woman.

He caught a fraction of his composure back to respond. "What makes you so magnificent that you believe you are entitled to the throne?" His expression implied that he knew she was, but he wanted to know how.

"I am the descendant of Alexander the Great," she said, and she needed to say no more.

He nodded his understanding, and considering the erotic, yet African look of her, he knew she was indeed a descendent of the great conqueror.

Chapter 8

The pharaoh relinquished his throne, and Cleopatra became the empress of Egypt. She liked this title better than Pharaohess. She threw exuberant parties for her people and her courtiers in celebration of her reign.

But only months after ascending to the throne, she received news of impending trouble from Rome. Seated in her greatest of great-grandfathers' library, consuming stories of all the greats, Jaffé came to her.

Jaffé made himself useful to the empress when she took her throne. He was the perfect courtier, who had been around longer than pharaohs of past. "Madam," he said.

"Yes, Jaffé?"

"A one Julius Caesar of Rome wishes to march on Egypt as Alexander did," he informed her. "He says he is the reincarnated Macedonian king. He has already conquered many countries and uses the same diplomacy as Alexander to win over the people in them."

This swaying of the people had also been in embedded in her from birth by her glorious queen mother. "Jaffé, gather up a chariot for me with my personal guards," she said.

"Are we planning to flee, madam?" he asked, which he felt was the only option.

"No, we head for Rome."

Jaffé, a short, slim old man, was shocked. His mouth dropped open, looking like a third eye because his eyes were just as wide. "Wh—wh—what?" he stammered. He had not lasted this long by moving rashly, and he was not about to do so now.

Cleopatra registered the fear in his voice and in his face. "You heard me,

Jaffé." She did not mean to repeat herself, especially to a cowardly old man. Like Jarmillah, she despised the fearful and had no patience for them.

"When do you want to leave?" he asked.

"We shall leave now," she said, standing up and putting down her book titled *I Am Ra*.

We? Jaffé thought. *Dung.*

She strutted out while Jaffé rushed about, yelling for the empress's private guards to mount up and the slaves to prepare her royal chariot, food, rugs, and the like for the journey to Rome.

*   *   *

They traveled for a great many weeks on the journey to Rome. But fortune would favor Cleopatra. On her way, she got word from a scout that Caesar was camped a few miles away and that within half a day they should be upon him.

Cleopatra told her entourage to settle in to allow the hell-raising sun to go down. Everyone, glad for the break, hurried and set up camp. Cleopatra went to a few of her guards and whispered to them. They nodded and left.

*   *   *

Julius Caesar was strategizing with his cousin Mark Anthony and his generals in a large tent when a soldier of his army came in. "Hail, Caesar," he greeted. Caesar looked up from a map of Egypt on the ground before him.

"A present has arrived for you from Cleopatra of Egypt, sire."

A present from Egypt, he thought. *It must be a token of the empress's esteem.*

He knew what an easy conquer Egypt would be with such a frail ruler. From what he had heard, she was the descendant of Alexander, so he had every intention on conquering her body for his own posterity. He could see the history books now with tales of his conquests of countries and concubines, like Alexander the Great, even conquering the conqueror's greatest of great-granddaughters.

"Send it in," he said. The soldier turned on his heels and left. Moments later, two jet-black, burly men came in carrying a plush rug, stitched by a designer who was blessed by the gods. Caesar nodded, admiring the richness of such a gift.

They nodded back at him and lowered the rug to their hips. Then, with a heave, they unfurled the rug in front of him. At the end of the rug rolled out Cleopatra, who rose and stood in front of Caesar in a fine see-through Egyptian silk. She seemed to be practically naked—every delicious curve of her body exposed. Caesar was in shock.

"I am Cleopatra," she simply stated.

He had intended to conquer her country first, and then her. But now he wanted to conquer countries just to be with her.

"And I am Caesar," he said, grabbing the hand she held out when he introduced himself. Caesar bent over and kissed the back of her hand. "It's a pleasure to meet you."

"I know," Cleopatra said. He did not know whether she meant she knew it was a pleasure to meet her or that she was acknowledging his pleasure meeting her. Either way, she was clearly aware of herself.

"Mama mia, you are the most beautiful woman I have ever seen," he told her.

Cleopatra just smiled, then winked at Mark Anthony. Mark Anthony was the next in line to rule over Rome. Even so, Cleopatra meant to enchant them both to ensure the peace of her country.

"Shall we walk," she said to Caesar.

"Yes," he said, then he turned to his men. "Cease everything." They looked at him in disbelief. One encounter with the enchantress and he was throwing in the towel. This was reckless, they thought.

"Can you accompany us, Mark Anthony?" she asked. Caesar frowned, wanting desperately to get her alone. All he needed was a tag-along to ruin the mood. Mark Anthony, instead of allowing Caesar to make his move alone, accepted. If looks could kill, Mark Anthony would have been dead cold from the look Caesar gave him.

The trio filed out of the tent and walked and chatted about the arts and philosophy under a star-studded night, avoiding all talk of war. Cleopatra only wanted to speak of pleasant matters. But war was far from either man's thoughts. She was smart, well read, and she served to captivate both men, while at the same time brewing up hate between them.

Cleopatra departed that night for Egypt, without fear of impending war and without giving up her diamond to either man. Caesar followed her.

In Egypt, she courted him, dazzling him with tales of Alexander the Great. Caesar was entranced with these tales and even imagined himself as Alexander in the process. At times when they were alone, he would make advances on the empress. When he did, she warded him off firmly with a smile. Caesar had a large fat nose with oddly shaped eyes and a cleft chin that gave him a cartoonish look. He was ugly, but to have such a Ra woman like Cleopatra at his side, he would feel like the most handsome man alive, as well as powerful.

But Cleopatra did not yield to him. In fact, she fell back from him and began to court Mark Anthony. Caesar was the most wise and volatile, so she leaned on the weaker link. Caesar made Mark Anthony look cute, and his long black hair gave him an attractive luster. Nonetheless, she couldn't care less if they were Adonis or not, as long as they served her purpose.

One day, she invited Mark Anthony to her palace for lunch.

Seated on her balcony, she fixed him over the table with a soft smile that aligned with her big, beautiful eyes. She said, "So, when are you going to rule over Rome?"

"When it's time," he responded.

She plucked out her lip, twitched her nose, and smiled. "When would that be? Because I am destined to be with rulers," she said in her hypnotic, musical voice.

Mark Anthony took her words as a hint of a marriage proposal. "Are you saying I am not good enough for you now?" he asked her.

She adjusted herself on the large silk, peacock-feather-stuffed cushion she sat on. "What's understood doesn't have to be said."

Mark Anthony sulked at her response. Then, when the realization of how simple it would be to become ruler of Rome came, he beamed with excitement. "I shall have you, mama mia," he declared and took his leave.

∗   ∗   ∗

Months later, Cleopatra heard of the death of Julius Caesar by a conspiracy authored by Mark Anthony. Almost immediately after, Mark Anthony died as well, for the same conspiracy. She had killed two lovebirds with one stone.

Cleopatra kept Egypt safe from Rome for the rest of her reign. Without battle, but all sway, Cleopatra became the first woman to rule unscathed during the patriarchal times.

Chapter 9

Modern-day Miami, Florida

Octave wanted to scream out to the highest octave. Julien had served him a blow. He did not mind sharing some of the company with his brother, but to cede to him control of the overall operation would bring about its certain death.

Days had passed since Julien gave his notice. Octave had been restless and spent more time in the office on his computer than at home. He was researching to find a loophole in Julien's petition.

He leaned back in his office chair and pinched the bridge of his nose. He was stressing hard about the matter with his brother. He would have no problem involving his brother in the family business—*if* he were responsible. But since he was not, this was a disaster in the making. The image of an impending hurricane approaching land served as a comparison to the matter at hand. The infrared color patterns on a meteorologist's screen signaled the foreboding of real disaster to come. And Julien's visit had been the foreboding of real disaster to come.

Octave shook his head and put his hands on his desk. By his left hand, he noticed a folder with a sticky note on top that read, "Predicted Sales—from Gwendolyn Thompson, Sales and Marketing." Silvia must have printed out the email when it came. He'd forgotten he had asked for this information—well, he didn't forget; he was put off by the situation with his brother. He grabbed the folder to look at its contents. He still needed to be aware of the company's progress. He still planned to run it, no matter what his brother was trying to do.

The predictions of project sales earnings were off the charts. There was a line of devices to develop and sell comprised of groundbreaking hot commodities. As Robert Kiyosaki said, the fastest way to get rich is to help others. And the products Armedia was planning to release did just that. Projected sales earnings of seventy million in the first quarter was a civil prediction that demonstrated profits without the colorful, excessive number of $300 million in sales. These charts embellished the sales that produced no dividends for stockholders. Who wants to see money they cannot touch?

"Mm-hmmm…" Octave nodded, smooching his lips and silently praising Gwendolyn's acuteness in her assessment. *She really did her thing*, he thought.

✳   ✳   ✳

But little did he know that was exactly what she wanted him to think, which was why she had signed her name on the documents. She refused to be used by Mr. Trent again. In the past, she had researched and typed up work, only to have him sign his name as the author, receiving credit for her hard work and creativity.

She grew tired of being passive and decided to assert herself. This wasn't a decision that came to her on its own. It was when she had seen the film *Hidden Figures*. Katherine Johnson, played by Taraji P. Henson, calculated the trajectory for space missions at NASA, but her supervisor didn't want her name on the documents. He refused to share credit with her when she should have been given all the acclaim. That story inspired Gwendolyn to not allow anyone to use her and her work—she would make herself *seen*.

Gwendolyn refused to keep her talents hidden, preventing her from elevating in her career. That was a no-no, and like Janelle Monáe's character Mary Jackson would say, "They can kiss my natural black ass."

✳   ✳   ✳

Octave grabbed his pen and began to take notes. A feeling of déjà vu hit him that reminded him of when he was studying to acquire the company—his birthright. What he learned had excited him and motivated him to want to run the company. Now, he jotted notes of projected sales, devising a plan to block his brother from taking over the CEO position.

He figured that if he could demonstrate before the board Julien's lack of knowledge in the company's growth, he could prevent him from taking the coveted CEO position. And the data he had before him was on point to prove it. No way his brother was privy of such sales projections. The outline of the products and marketing was so detailed that Octave knew that if Julien were to see it, he'd be spending money that wasn't even there. Ms. Thompson was a beast at date prediction.

Octave had thought the same of Mr. Trent when he was first seeking his birthright. Mr. Trent's practical, yet instructive summary of the company's core purpose had been informative and especially beneficial to his endeavor. But this time, it was Gwendolyn's work that would help him.

Octave finished his notes and organized them to compose his presentation.

Chapter 10

Spain, 1400s

"Isabella! ISABELLA MIA SAUREZ!" Gloria Saurez called out to her daughter, the wanderer.

The little Latina girl was lying by a pond, away from her family's manor, lost in her thoughts. The grass next to the pond was so green that it appeared to be glowing. Isabella lay in this rich grass with even richer thoughts, oblivious to the bugs that stalked around her, inching closer and closer to make war with the overgrown insect that dared to invade their domain.

Isabella was thinking of grandeur. She was born a princess, destined to be queen, but she was confused as to how her father—the living, breathing Latin force—was not a king. Wouldn't she have to be the daughter of a king to be a princess? Or was she the daughter of a man who loved her like a princess? Either way makes her a princess, right?

Poor Papi. She wished at times he was around. She remembered his ways of talking—big dreams, small goals, and no ambition.

At least that was what her mami used to say about him. Isabella felt her father was of the visionary class. The class of people who see things so real that they can feel it, taste it, and every other way sense it, but they just cannot get to it. She believed that if you could see it, you could get it. However, her mami said that was like grabbing a raging bull—you are liable to be tossed, falling flat on your culo.

Isabella heard her mother and quickly rose. If her mother knew she had wandered off so far from the manor, she would kill her. Gloria feared bandits kidnapping her and holding her for ransom. And knowing the present king would not pay for his niece's return, she would surely die.

Isabella jumped up and ran barefoot toward the manor. When she got close, she yelled out, "Coming, Mami!" She arrived at her doorstep, gasping for air, where her mother awaited her.

"You think you can convince me that you were close by with the way you are panting like a tired bull?" Gloria asked her.

Isabella tried to catch her breath, then she looked up at her tall, elegant mother, whose forehead showed worry lines but whose mouth wore a hint of a smile. "I was playing," Isabella said—a good response because a child of twelve can play in a way that equaled running a marathon.

"Very well then, mija." Her mother took her words for what they were worth. "Go freshen up and get ready for supper."

*   *   *

At the dinner table, enjoying a ravishing Spanish meal, Gloria peered at her daughter, who seemed to have stopped growing at age eleven. She wondered what type of woman she would be at such a small stature. Would she be the first of the Saurez women to become queen of Spain? Isabella was a headstrong girl with the wandering spirit of her father. The visionary type that was rare for women of their times. *What type of woman dwells on things outside of tradition?*

Gloria mentally sighed. Maybe times were changing. The queen of England had her time of building a vision for her country, but those gents in England had silver tongues to manipulate their women. Who was to say her decisions were her own?

Gloria shook her head in distaste at these thoughts. Isabella, placing a fork with a chunk of roast chicken in her mouth, saw her mother's gesture, and asked, "Qué pasa? What is wrong, Mami?"

"De nada, mija," Gloria said, "I was just thinking about something."

"Something like what?" Isabella pressed on, eager to engage in an adult conversation that would potentially leave her feeling intelligent or important.

Gloria considered her daughter's question. She thought of brushing her off, or simply making up a *something*. But why not let her daughter know what the world has in store for her—the role she must play in this man's world. Isabella would be eligible for marriage in a few more years, and she had that *estúpido* imagination like her father that Gloria despised. It was time for her daughter to face reality.

"Mija," Gloria told her, "I was thinking about the queen of England."

"The Queen of England," Isabella parroted.

"Yes, I wondered, did she really have the power she willed, or was it her power by a man's will?"

Baffled, Isabella asked, "What does that mean?"

"It means that a woman's role is under a man's. She must be respectful to him. This is to stop the girl's foolish imaginings. Big dreams lead to bad days when you don't reach them."

"Papi said that every dream is realized when you attempt to awaken it."

Her daughter's response infuriated her. "Where did that get him?" Gloria shook her head roughly. "No fucking where. Isabella, women are not men, who go imagining nonsense. For them, it is foolish, but for us, it is a downright abomination."

"So, we don't *think, we do?*" Isabella asked sarcastically. "Being subservient isn't an abomination?"

"You miss the point," Gloria said. Her daughter's rational response quelled her anger.

"No, Mami. I get the point," she said. "I just don't like it."

Gloria slowly shook her head as she watched her daughter painfully swallow the reality of life. "It is just the way it is, mija," she said after a moment.

"It is not *my* way, Mami," Isabella declared. Her mother shook her head, but Isabella continued. "And it will never be. If I want my own thoughts heard or heeded, I will use my voice. And if my master—my husband doesn't like it, I will run away from him."

Her mother gasped. "Isabella Mia Saurez, do not speak blasphemy. A marriage is anointed by God."

"That makes sense." Isabella rolled her eyes. "It must be a man-god who would subject a woman to such a fate," Isabella retorted.

"Now you surely speak blasphemy."

"Why is that?"

"Evita ate of the tree—"

"So did Adam," Isabella cut her off, "but you don't see his male offspring as slaves to us, do you?" Isabella didn't wait for a response. "I don't see how I must pay for something I didn't do. And I cannot see a caring God making me either.

"Papi said his papa was a Moor, who in Africa worshipped a wise, loving woman that we in Spain call the Black Madonna. She is who people prayed to and asked for guidance and protection. If the curse of Evita is true, why would God give a woman such power?

"The Africans know that women are an equal force to men and address them as so. And it is that rare type of woman, who breaks from tradition and believes in herself, with no help or promotion from society, who becomes a force to be reckoned with. She makes history *her* story.

"And I do believe the queen of England is one of those women," Isabella said, matter of fact.

"The women you speak of are witches, not queens," Gloria said.

"Then I want to be a witch," Isabella said, nodding for emphasis.

Gloria's eyes clouded with fear. "My child, witches are bad."

To her mother's chagrin, she responded, "Then I would be a badass witch."

"You will be married soon, Isabella. You can't afford not to be."

"I do not oppose marriage, Mami. I just do not see myself leaning back and staying quiet when I want to come forward and say something. And I'll be damned if my husband won't let me."

Chapter 11

Twelve years later

Christopher Columbus was led before the sovereigns inside the throne room of the castle. The king sat in all his majesty on his throne to the right of his queen. Christopher bowed to both, one at a time. The breath almost left him at the sight of the queen. Queen Isabella. The beautiful Spanish queen. She was small in stature, slender yet shapely as a woman. Her beauty was of its own. Her face looked to be carved by the hands of a divine, meticulous artist.

Her nose was small but firmly shaped, lining up perfectly with her mahogany eyes, which, when a man investigated them, he could not help but crave their insight. Her lips were neither thin nor plump, but a perfect symmetrical width and thickness that complemented her African and Indo-European heritage. Freckles outlining her cheeks reminded one of a delectable ice cream with sprinkles over top. The blemishes were the only proof that the queen was human.

Christopher had travelled far and wide looking for financial backers for his expedition. He'd thought of a new way to reach Asia to trade in a convenience that would make him and his investors rich in the process. Plus, undiscovered land along the way was sure to contain untapped resources and perhaps even gold.

The king, who had already heard about this wild man's fool ideas, was already planning to turn him down. He stared at him with hawk eyes under furry eyebrows.

"Sire, if I may?" Christopher asked.

"Go on," the king answered.

"I have an idea that I wish to share with your highness," Christopher began. "The world as we know it is not flat but round. I believe that if we travel west, we can reach the East faster and without encountering those savage barbarians, losing less and gaining much."

"And what do you propose?" the king asked. He was entertaining himself with this jester of a man.

"By sailing west, we create a new route to reach Asia and possibly discover new land."

"That sounds simple enough, but why do I think the price would not be worthwhile?"

Christopher, who was sweating in his tights and triple-breast wool jacket, scratched his head. "Well, sire, I need three fully manned ships with supplies—food, gunpowder, kerosene, and an so on."

"In summation, you need a fully financed voyage?" the king interjected.

"Yes, sire," Christopher boldly responded.

"And what would be the benefit to the royal treasury?"

Christopher's beady eyes widened, and his pudgy neck seemed to roll then jiggle at the question. "Sire, I guarantee you a portion of the wealth and land declared in the name of your highness." Christopher planned to keep twenty percent, which he believed would be a fortune in years to come.

The king's hawk eyes clouded over with menace. The nerve of this imbecile to ask him to fully finance his expedition, then offer him only "a portion." He should cast him down to the dungeon and eighty lashes for his blatant disrespect.

But he was bold and obviously *estupido*, so the king fury's subsided as fast as it came. No more jesting though. It was time to send the buffoon away.

"I am not interested," he said flatly.

Just as Christopher's shoulders slumped from the rejection, the queen spoke up. "But I *am* interested."

The king's head snapped toward his wife, looking at her in disbelief. She went on, "I think we can benefit greatly," she said to her husband. He frowned. "At a more respectful agreement, though."

The king sighed. He could not fathom allowing this imbecile to get off on a free paradise cruise at his expense. He had no faith in the possibility of a western route to Asia, nor any grand discovery of treasure lands. But most importantly, he knew not to oppose his wife, the queen, no matter the consequences.

Queen Isabella had established herself in the Spanish kingdom years ago. The king gave her free reign of the kingdom that she demanded. Not to decorate or dominate the servants like other queens of the day, but she ruled over the whole kingdom. Isabella commanded the knights and was the bearer of grievances of the king's subjects, which were in fact her subjects.

Isabella equally ruled over Spain with her husband, realizing both her mother's dream of a Suarez woman becoming queen and her own of being a ruling queen. Isabella knew her husband would not agree to back a wild dream because, like many men, he lacked imagination. But she saw potential in Columbus's idea, and from conversing with her subjects, she'd heard stories of visitors from lands that were unknown at the time.

Some of these lands, she'd heard, had their share of treasures. So the queen knew what Christopher Columbus claimed was perhaps possible. Plus, this anxious man reminded her of her imaginative father, whom she'd always taken seriously. Allowing this man to realize his dream would be like paying homage to her father.

"That's very gracious, my queen," Christopher said. "What do you prefer?"

"We finance the expedition and grant royal favor to you and your family forever."

This did not sound fair to him, but he was anxious to explore the world. Besides, the queen, here in Spain, could not possibly know what he would find out there in the sea.

"Thank you, your highness," he accepted.

"You are to prepare for sailing immediately. See my marshal for everything needed for the voyage," she instructed.

"Yes, your highness," he said.

"You are dismissed."

Christopher Columbus hurried out with Queen Isabella's blessing to make history—a history that would leave out her part in the story for centuries to come.

Chapter 12

Modern-day Miami, Florida

Not a day goes by without a monkey wrench thrown in the works, Gwendolyn thought. She would have to polish up this and sprinkle that, but these details came with being a hands-on woman in her line of work. And no woman wanted to go out in the world with her nails undone. "Ugh," she sighed, but not from frustration.

Gwendolyn succumbed to the theatrics, but she loved getting the job done. It was what she was born to do. She did not think anybody could cover for her—at least not at her job. She made a note to herself that when she was CEO, she wouldn't impose on her employees; but she was determined to prepare the itinerary to such a specific degree that each department would run as if she were there in each one at the same time.

The phone on her desk rang. She smiled at the noise, priding herself on being able to do two things at once. She was not conceited, she didn't think, but confident. And like Demi, she asked herself, "What's wrong with being confident?"

She answered the phone with a business-like "Hello, Ms. Thompson here."

After a brief pause from hearing her voice again, Octave said, "Yes, this is Octave Royal. I wanted to thank you for the papers you sent. They were beautiful." *Beautiful? That's a strong assessment of some papers,* he thought.

Was he laying down game? It had been a week since she'd emailed the documents, and she knew such communications at the multibillion-dollar corporation were delivered by the best servers money could buy; the mail reaches its destination in split seconds. But here he was thanking her a week later. The way he had been pressing for the information, she had thought he would have reviewed it ASAP. His urgency must have been a show of authority. The nerve of him.

"All right, sir," she said. "Is there anything else you need?"

"Um," The question caught him off guard, as well as the formal way she addressed him after he had used the word *beautiful.* He wanted her to be pleased by the compliment, or at least thankful for it. Maybe his selfish desire was transparent, and she was put off by his praise, reading into his intent.

But that is not what he intended. But *what did you intend?* he asked himself. He shook his head, restraining from blowing air and rattling his jaws like a canine. A desperate dog would probably not sit well with her.

"No," he finally said.

"Okay, sir," she said. "Bye." She hung up. He still cradled the phone as if she were still on the line. He wanted to say more, but it was too late.

Or was it? He pressed the redial button.

She picked up. "Hello, Ms. Thompson," he heard her say, but he was stuck for a moment. Butterflies suddenly invaded his stomach. His palms started to sweat.

"I was thinking," he began, "would you like to have lunch with me?"

Hell to the no, she thought, but said, "I'm booked for the day. Maybe some other time."

He thought about pressing on but did not want to make himself seem thirsty. "Okay, then, but did you hear me when I said I liked her prognosis?"

Now I am deaf apparently. "Yes, I did," she lied.

He tried to think of a response that would appeal to her, but nothing came to mind. "All right, Gwen—um, Ms. Thompson."

Gwendolyn wanted to hang up without responding but settled for "Mm-hm." Then she hung up. She'd caught him catching himself from calling her by her first name. Like they were on a first-name basis. Mr. Trent tried her the same. This had to be a bomb drop for sexual harassment in the work force.

A build-up it must be, as if superiors calling a woman employee by her first name implied intimacy. And if she failed to correct him, it hinted to him that she was down with it. "It" being the bullshit sexual overtures and obnoxious flirting. She would have to be a silly ho to fall for something like that. That was why she was quick to check Mr. Trent about addressing her informally. However, she did not mind him or any male colleague addressing her by her full name, which was appropriate.

She pushed the phone away and went back to doing her job. *Hombre estúpido,* she thought.

Chapter 13

Colonial America
New England Territories

"I hate being here," Matilda said, seated in front of a big mirror that sat on top of her bedroom dresser, brushing her long blonde hair. She stopped brushing and looked in the mirror at the woman behind her. "Shareka, why are men so impossible?"

"I'sa have no idea, madam," Shareka said. She was used to being the ear for her mistress. Shareka, like every obedient slave at the time, was in the business of slave laborer and listener.

"Well, I can be careless about my chores," Matilda spat, then resumed brushing her hair. After a moment, Matilda stopped, shook her head, and set the brush on the dresser. "You have no idea? I know that's a lie, Shareka," she said, staring at the young woman in the mirror whose eyes were soft ebony, like doves. Matilda furrowed her brows. Shareka remained silent.

When Shareka did not respond, Matilda turned to the side to face her. "What's wrong? I was expecting the sage advice that you have bestowed upon me for years. Now here you are, quiet as a monk. Something must be wrong."

Shareka turned from her and stared off. Matilda stood up and thrust her face in front of Shareka's. "What's wrong?"

"Now…" Shareka's voice trailed off. She did not want to lie to her mistress, but she regretted the truth.

Her eyes moistened as Matilda stared into them, awaiting a response. The tears made Matilda feel bad about demanding Shareka to reveal her feelings to her without considering those feelings.

"I am sorry, Shareka," she exclaimed. Then she did the unthinkable during those times—she hugged her. Shareka hugged her back tightly. Matilda tightened her embrace in response, anxious to console her slave, her confidante, her friend, her sister.

Shareka and Matilda had known each other all their lives. They were born on the same hot, muggy summer day, the last day of August, twenty-six years ago. Matilda's father, Joe Clark, owned Shareka's mother, Maybel, and so she took his last name, as was tradition. Shareka lived out in the shack with her mother and the other slaves, but she was allowed entry in the master's house because her mother was his favorite.

Shareka grew up fast and was schooled by her mother and the other slave women in the do's and don'ts of the white-ruled world. (They refused to call it a "white man's world.") They were brought up as the caregivers and backbone of the Black household, the ruling beings of their world. Shareka was equipped with the wisdom and shrewdness that were innate to Black women, who had an instinctive perception of things and a broad view on life that was inherent.

Hence the homegrown remedies and concoctions for every kind of ailment. It was with this knowledge that, when Matilda—now head of the house after her parents' death—was sick, Shareka concocted an herbal tea remedy used for colds and congestion—an old remedy used by Black folks. She brewed the tea, then gave it to Matilda, who immediately, yet gradually, began to recover. Matilda begged Shareka for the ingredients for the healing tea when she needed it, and Shareka humbly obliged.

Sure enough, Matilda had a need for the healing tea when her sister-in-law's son became ill. Tracy was visiting with her husband for the holidays when she told her about her son. After hearing this, Matilda immediately took charge of the situation, imitating Shareka's pensive, calm manner in the process. Tracy watched her and was awed by her serene confidence. It was as if she knew she would heal her son. Days after the sick child drank the herbal tea, he was healed.

Matilda's sister-in-law told her husband and everyone else about it. This was the beginning of the trouble. Shareka hated herself for it. The healing herbal tea was what the townspeople used to accuse Matilda of witchcraft. Well, that and her exceptional intelligence convicted her.

The use of Shareka's counsel in marital matters and more were an asset. Matilda was learned in humanities through literature, but she was given experienced knowledge of humanity through Shareka from her observant, intuitive wisdom.

Shareka knew it was her fault, but what she did not know was how to make it right for her mistress. It had been an epidemic throughout the European nations—to stake and burn women who were convicted of being witches. All these women were not guilty of the charge, however. Of course, some were true witches, and a few were budding witches, but none deserved the fate they received. More often than not, Black women were the confidantes and teachers of the accused white women.

They all pledged to come together in a secret union to prevent more deaths. They cared about these white women and felt guilty for their fate. The intertwining of cultures and races was sure to cause confusion, or imitation. It was inevitable that each culture adopted the ways of the other. The Africans who were enslaved were forced to adopt the European ways of their masters' and vice versa.

In the African culture, the woman was the matriarch, the backbone, the decision-making queen. The patriarch leanings were more so forced upon their world through the European men who were frustrated and possibly envious of the reigning queens of the African nations. And the Africans, referred to as negroes, were still living a matriarchal existence that in modern times would be referred to "Big Mama's" tradition, describing the dominant woman of the household.

The white women took to this tradition because buried beneath the forcefully inculcated lady of decency–a subservient, dependable being— was fire. A fire that was so hot that it could melt gold. Melting it into a crown.

They began congregating with one another, then secretly congregating with Black women. And they were exposed to the hot queen within them, gaining backbone to inevitably recognize their queenliness. *Queenly* was what one would call a headstrong woman—opinionated and confident.

And during medieval times, a woman who was not a subservient doormat was a threat. Women who were capable to rule—well, the insecure, effeminate men of the day were not having it. As a result, they made up diabolical tall tales, warning of the whims of a woman. To be smart and caring in the apothecary fashion was evil. A woman who was willing to kill kids instead of bearing them. But really, they would rather her to make babies then to have a mind of her own.

Any type of woman who did not meet their expectation was a witch.

Shareka had no choice. She had to tell Matilda what was happening.

"Madam," she began in her accented English. "Ya husband is at a meeting with the townspeople."

"I know that," she said. "I didn't need you for that information."

Shareka shook her head. "Please, let me finish?" Matilda nodded, but felt honeybees begin to swarm in her stomach. "They think you'sa witch."

"A witch, what?" she asked, confused.

"Ya husband and some other men are planning to come arrest ya and hold ya on trial for being a witch," Shareka cried.

"Oh, my," was all Matilda could say to that. A witch trial, she knew, was torture.

Shareka tried to think of any way to prevent such a fate for her mistress, but she fell short of ideas. All she knew to do was to pack Matilda up and leave. Shareka wanted to allow her to live her normal life, but that was impossible now.

"You's must leave, me lady, before it's too late."

"But why do they think I am a witch?" she asked fearfully.

"They'sa know ya husband is telling 'em about the healing of ya nephew and how outspoken and brilliant ya is," Shareka explained. But she held back the real reason, which was that her husband was having an affair with a younger woman and wanted out of their marriage so he could marry her.

Labeling his wife an evil witch was the best way to get Matilda out of the way. The dirty bastard. Tears filled Matilda's eyes, then they filled Shareka's eyes like a contagious reaction, until they all spilled out. Matilda reached out and grabbed Shareka's dress, then leaned her head on her shoulder and began bawling. When her crying subsided, her agony was reduced to moaning.

Between sniffles, she asked Shareka, "Why me?"

"It ain't cha fault," Shareka consoled her. Fault finding was not up for consideration; escaping was. How was Matilda to get out of this situation alive and unscratched?

"We'sa must go now," Shareka said, after a moment. Matilda looked up at her as Shareka wiped the tears off her cheeks.

"We?" she said.

"We," Shareka repeated.

Matilda hugged her friend. "You are too good to me."

Shareka did not respond but broke their embrace. She grabbed Matilda by her shoulders and said, "Look at me." Matilda saw the seriousness in Shareka's ebony eyes. "We'sa have to go now while it's still daylight."

The witch hunters liked to stalk at night, drawing on the mysticism of a witch trial under pale moonlight.

"Also, me lady, ya gonna endure a lot of hardship once night falls," she warned her. "Ya can move like a lady in the light, butcha gotta move like a scavenger at night."

Matilda nodded. "Where would we go?"

"Away from here."

Chapter 14

They traveled for days, moving only at night. In the daytime, Shareka and Matilda would hide in caves or deep in the forest. The latter was ironic since, here they were, running because Matilda was accused of being a witch, yet hiding in the very place witches were known to dwell.

Daylight now prominent, they laid low in the forest. Sitting on two large tree trunks, Matilda fluffed her hair and asked Shareka, "How do I look?" Shareka peered at her mistress. Matilda's hair was knotted up and disheveled.

She looked a mess. Even her makeup was fading away, the dark blush she'd applied before they left was rubbed out, exposing the pale skin that was common to New Englanders.

Shareka smiled at her, then said, "Ya beautiful, me lady."

Matilda shook her head. "You're too good to me, my sister," she said. "You know good and well I look like a white, hot mess." They burst out laughing. When the laughing subsided, Shareka gazed upon her with a look that made Matilda start to feel uncomfortable.

"Wh—what's the matter?" she asked timidly.

Shareka stared on for a few more seconds before speaking. "I'sa told ya from the beginning of our journey that you'sa face hardship."

"I know that, I was—"

Shareka cut her off. "But I'sa telling ya that the look of ya is nowhere near what we'sa left behind. I'sa know you'sa making light of the situation, but sometimes we try to escape what's real. That's not what we'sa need right now, Matilda."

Matilda did not know if she was supposed to respond or not, so she remained silent and nodded pensively.

"I'sa don't lie when I'sa say ya beautiful," Shareka said. "Under the circumstances, the way you'sa stayed calm shows ya stability of mind—ya strength. And that's beautiful, me sister."

Matilda smiled and reached out to her. Breaking their embrace, Shareka said, "But far as ya looks go, ya look like She-Ra."

Matilda cocked her head. "Who is that?"

"A warrior princess from ya barbaric ancestry, who was said to play the flute and was so deft with the sword that they'sa said she was Ra. That saying became her name—She-Ra. With her long golden locks hanging loose during battle, she'sa never bound it or wore it up. Her hair was her crown. Ya know, like lions' hair?"

"You think I'm Ra?" Matilda asked.

"I know ya is," she said. This served to lift Matilda's spirits because she was feeling homesick.

She wanted desperately for her life to go back to normal—even playing the subservient wife. But Shareka's verbal chastisement and her comparison to She-Ra made her feel Ra.

"Thank you, my sister."

"That's what I'sa here fo'," Shareka said, then she looked up to the sky. "The sun is 'bout to set. We are almost there, so we move at sunset and should arrive at sunrise."

"Almost there" had been a recurring mantra from Shareka since they set off on their journey. Matilda had no idea where there was.

"Where is there?" she asked.

Shareka just shook her head. "You'sa know when we'sa get there," she said.

Matilda could not help feeling that Shareka was overly optimistic about their journey and was only saying "almost there" to make her feel good. But that was not the case. Shareka intentionally held back from disclosing their destination in case Matilda was captured and forced to expose it.

*   *   *

Night fell and they journeyed on, barefoot through the forest. They'd lost their shoes miles back, and it was a good thing it was summer. In the New England winter, the snow and ice would have them catching frost bite and possibly freezing to death.

The night sky was filled with stars that, like peeping Toms, peered down from the tops of the trees at the women as they walked. The night was gloomy with frightening forest sounds creating an eerie song that accompanied them on their journey. Matilda wished she were a witch, able to cast a spell that would transport them to the unknown there Shareka kept talking about. She heard the noises of the dark forest—the cracking of tree branches and rustling of leaves.

It was as if a bear were stalking them—or worse, Bigfoot. She had heard plenty of tales of man-eating sasquatches from the natives and shuddered in a cold fear at the thought of an encounter with such a creature. She picked up her step behind Shareka.

After hours of walking, they came to the edge of the forest. An owl could be heard repeatedly asking, "Who?" as if it were a demanding gatekeeper. Shareka stopped and peered into the distance. Matilda stopped as well, then looked at Shareka.

Shareka turned to her and said, "We'sa here."

Here? Matilda thought. "You mean *here* as in *there?*" she asked hopefully.

Shareka nodded. "C'mon," she said and scurried off. Matilda hurriedly followed.

A ways farther were a cluster of lampposts lit by kerosene. Matilda saw them and was awed. It was like discovering a secret city in the woods. As they walked forward, they came across log cabins and stone structures that made up a small village.

Peering out of the windows of the houses were women of all ages and races. "Shareka's here!" someone yelled. Women filed out of the houses and some came from around the backs of the houses until the dirt road was filled with women. They all wore black. Black dresses, black hats, and some even carried black bags. It looked like a witch haven. But the wardrobe was necessary to blend in with the shadowy forest, to remain undiscovered by the wrong people—witch hunters.

The women gathered around the two newcomers, chattering loudly. Then, when they had surrounded them, they grew silent and parted. An elderly Black woman with long white hair stood before them, staring with unblinking eyes that made Matilda nervous.

"Welcome, me lady," she said, bowing her head.

"It is always a pleasure to be welcomed, me sister," Shareka said. Matilda's head snapped toward Shareka in surprise. She had thought that the woman was talking to her—"me lady"—but she was in fact addressing Shareka.

Then, more shocking was the tone and diction of Shareka's voice; she sounded…authoritative.

"Is this our sister?" the elderly woman asked.

"Yes, Theresa, this is Matilda." The elderly woman shuffled forward, eying Matilda again with that same unnerving, unblinking stare. Then she reached out and hugged them both in greeting.

Chapter 15

Later that day, after bathing and ridding themselves of their ragged dresses and donning the customary black dresses of the village, Shareka and Matilda sat out in the clearing.

Matilda watched the women go about their normal routines, she supposed, when she noticed two women holding hands and walking toward the forest. One of the women she at first thought was a man because her hair was cut short. It was a new style adopted by the military, which insisted that men's long hair was an encumbrance in combat. The generals made it the army's policy for all soldiers to wear short hair.

The woman was slim with a militant posture and a femininity that made her seem elegantly roguish. The women stopped and looked at each other with such an intense, loving expression that to Matilda it seemed like they were in their own world. Then they kissed. Matilda's brows rose in surprise, but a part of her had known the kiss was coming.

She was at a loss for thought. Her brain froze to digest what she had just witnessed. She processed the evils that were associated with such women, inculcated in her mind by her family and society while growing up.

This was the first time she had seen such a romance between women. However, she had read about them. One was Sappho, the Greek poet from Lesbos, an island where such women lived. This was the origin of the term *lesbian,* which was what they called themselves. Sappho wrote that the love of two women is the ultimate love. But in Matilda's society, this ultimate love was considered demonic. She shook her head, thinking how small-minded people could be.

A woman who was smart enough to read and think on her own was considered an evil witch, and women who loved one another, or who preferred the company of other women, were demonic. But here was a village of women living together in harmony—no, living in love—and not caring what the world outside thought of them standing fast with one another. This place, Matilda thought, was like an enchanted forest. But there was not any mysticism about it; it was real.

The flakes and fakes, like her bastard husband, giving off foolery for reality to suit their own needs of unsophisticated understanding, gave rise to the mysticism and charges of witchcraft. Here was a place where women could think on their own and love how they pleased with no misgivings or regrets. They loved who they were and couldn't care less about what the outside world thought.

But would the world catch on or stay planted in their own bullshit?

"How are you, me sister?" Shareka asked.

Matilda took a moment to consider her question. "I am fine," she began, "but what is this place and how is it that you are…?" She trailed off, unable to put into words the way Shareka had been treated like a queen. It was as though she were the head of this tribe.

Now her thoughts trailed off. Matilda could not decide who these women were. She did not even know if her friend was who she had thought.

Shareka smiled. "I am who I am, and they are who they are."

That was a vague response, Matilda thought. She scrunched her face. "What?"

"This is the Ring."

"Oh, that's what it is," Matilda said, rolling her eyes. "Well, that explains everything." Shareka laughed.

"It isn't funny, Shareka. I come here to find out that the woman I have known my whole life is some type of badass witch over a village of witches. That is not some funny business," Matilda said indignantly.

"I understand where you are coming from, but we are here," Shareka told her, then looked her deep in her eye. "We'sa women, and we'sa here for each other. I'sa here for you."

She reached out and grabbed Matilda's hand. "The Ring is a circle of women, which is the completion of the earth. We'sa here for each other, and we'sa going to be here always, even when times get hard. Our history goes back. A history of powerful women linked to one another throughout the ages to form womankind."

Matilda thought about what Shareka said about her resemblance to She-Ra yesterday. Was she truly aligned with such a powerful woman, or even aligned with other women of the same ilk?

"Yes, you'sa is," Shareka said.

Matilda's eyes widened, and she snatched her hand away from her. "Did you just read my mind?"

Shareka frowned. "What?"

"Did you know what I was thinking?" Matilda asked anxiously.

"No, silly. I'sa finishing my story," Shareka said, then chuckled.

Matilda recalled the conversation, and that made sense. Feeling silly, she said, "Oh, I was just thinking about what you said, and your words confirmed my thoughts."

"I'm glad," Shareka said. "Besides, I'sa know ya like I'sa know myself."

"I wish I knew you like that."

A hurt expression formed on Shareka's face. "Ya do know me, and you's always have."

Matilda looked around the Ring village and thought about the women— how they looked up to Shareka, her friend, her sister. Then she thought, *No, sister, I do not.*

"Ya don't know them, so you'sa think there's more to me. But I's always been me," Shareka explained. "In due time, they'sa know ya, too, and they's address ya as if you'sa badass witch of the village. Because we's all come from a royal lineage of extraordinary women."

"I am almost certain you read my mind this time," Matilda said accusingly. Shareka smiled.

Chapter 16

Modern-day Miami, Florida

The day after phoning Gwendolyn, Octave was once again seated at his office desk, feeling down. He had considered calling in and telling Silvia to reschedule any appointments he had for the day and staying home. He felt drained. This draining feeling was new to him. However, he knew the cause was Gwendolyn. He did not understand why she was offended by him praising her work. Maybe she had issues.

Yeah, that might be the case. She might be one of those bag ladies—a drama queen. Whatever she was, he *wanted to be part of her*. Wanted to be part of her—the thought echoed in his mind. What did that mean? Was it that he was horny, or was it her no-nonsense attitude? His encounter with her was brief, so he could not understand where these feelings came from. He had been involved with a few women in the past, but nothing major far as commitment goes.

He liked them, but never to the point of *wanting* them. Octave shook his head at the thought of what he wanted. Did that mean he *wanted* Gwendolyn? That was a silly thought, he felt, because he did not even know her. He did not think he was the type to thirst for companionship. He was more concerned with pursuing his dreams than living in romantic fantasies. The matter with Gwendolyn, he felt, was remorse. He was feeling guilty for offending her and wanted to make amends. That was what it had to be.

He shrugged, mentally dismissing the deep feelings as misinterpreted guilt. Then he grabbed his desk phone, dialed up a few numbers, and leaned back in his chair as the phone rang.

After a couple rings, a woman answered. "Hello?" Her "hello" was more so a question than a greeting.

"This is Mr. Royal. I'm sorry to bother you, Cheryl."

Cheryl was the general secretary for the company, the go-between for the board members, who were heads of their own companies, founders, and CEOs. "No, no, sir, you're not," she said. "How can I help you?"

"I'm planning to call an earlier board meeting."

"Okay."

"It would be for…." He checked his schedule. Thursday he was free, and it was Tuesday. Two days. "Thursday, please."

"Yes, sir," she said. "Will that be all?"

He thought about it for a moment and said, "Yes, Cheryl, that's all. Have a nice one."

"You too, sir," Cheryl said. "Bye."

"Bye," he sounded off. He cradled the phone before hanging it up. The die was cast. He would have to lay down his reason for not allowing his brother to lead the corporation or tear it down. The convincing would have to be professional. He could not go into how Julien stole a bicycle and cheated on his SATs when he was a teenager. Petty personal allegations would not fly. He would have to point out serious professional flaws.

Why Julien was not fit for the CEO position…. His ace in the hole was Gwendolyn's data. He composed a relevant argument from it. He would have to wait to see whether it would be enough to sway the board or not. Knowing Julien like he knew himself, he knew his brother would not take it lying down. Julien was bound to have his own reasons for why he was fit for the job.

Octave could only hope that whatever his brother's reason was, it was weak. Better yet, maybe the whole "Mr. CEO" was a passing fancy of Julien's, and he really did not intend to follow through with it. Perhaps he'd acted on an impulsive desire that he later realized was ridiculous.

All of the above Octave knew to be wishful thinking. Julien was a bona fide fuck-up, but he was also a Royal. It was in their DNA to be achievers, even overachievers; therefore, he had best be on point and ready for a fight.

*   *   *

Gwendolyn was ready for a fight. She felt angry for nothing. And angry for nothing made a person want to take that anger out on *something*. What had her upset was the product release of a new Mattel-corroborated toy communication device that posed as both phone and tablet for kids ages four through nine. The Kidbizz it was called.

The Kidbizz was a worthy product that was sure to fly off the shelves once in stores. The delay was nothing major, but she still was upset. Although, she did not really want to fight anyone. She was just frustrated.

She considered taking the rest of the day off but decided against it. What she needed was to vent. She pulled out her cellphone and touched the screen a couple times to call Amanda. Amanda Kusevich had been her best friend since the red-light/green-light days. They had gone from playing kid games to teenage girl woes to grown woman business.

Amanda had been the only white girl at the predominantly Black and Latino public schools in Liberty City. She was one of a few white girls Gwendolyn knew who grew up around Blacks but still maintained her identity. She was hip, but she was white. She was not a white girl who acted Black, making her a "yellow bone." Although, she did tend to use slang, and she would cuss out—not curse—anybody who got her time wrong, like a Black girl would. She was a slim, petite woman, who wore glasses, but she took no nonsense from anybody.

One ring and Amanda picked up. "Hi, you?" she asked. Amanda had to be the only one in the world who could make "hi" sound like "how," while still pronouncing it "hi."

"Not too good," Gwendolyn responded. "You want to do lunch?"

Amanda looked at her watch. It was a quarter after ten. "Meet me at Wingstop."

"Okay, sweetheart," Gwendolyn said, smiling at her friend's likability. Amanda neither protested nor quizzed her over the phone about why she wanted to meet.

"You're buying," Amanda said and clicked off.

"Or she just wanted a free meal," Gwendolyn said out loud, smiling.

At Wingstop, they took their meals out to Amanda's SUV, a Cadillac Escalade. They sat in the spacious backseat, Styrofoam plates of food in their laps while they got their grub on with the paper bag it came in between them.

Gwendolyn looked over at her friend and caught her scarfing down chicken wings one after another. She looked her up and down, trying to figure out where all that food was going. Amanda was model-slim. "Girl, your food must go to your brain."

"I was thinking the same," Amanda said. "I am pretty smart." They laughed. "But," Amanda said, taking a bite out of another chicken wing. "What's going on with you?"

"Girl, I am tired," she said. Amanda chewed with an "I-am-listening" expression. "Tired of being mistreated, used, and unappreciated."

"Work, huh?"

She inhaled deeply and exhaled hard before continuing. "I'm trying to stick through the bullshit, but nothing seems to fall in place. The Kidbizz is supposed to be ready and available for wholesale, plus shipped to some of our stores, but they had to delay the release.

"I know if I were the CEO, I wouldn't let that slide. In fact, it would not even go down like that, period. Mr. Quincy is not doing shit. If I were the boss, I would not let products get delayed after my people's thorough effort to help me get money. The company sells a product, then the stocks rise, plus bonuses.

"But besides the money, I'd want to be the best at what I do." Gwendolyn finally stopped from what seemed like a one-breath rant.

Amanda was still stuffing down chicken, taking another bite, nodding, and humming, "Mm-hmm." She really did not want to give any feedback yet. She knew Gwendolyn had already worked everything out in her mind and was merely venting.

"But there's another stockholders meeting coming up, and I plan to voice my opinion on the matter at hand," Gwendolyn said, noticing Amanda still nodding and gnawing on a chicken wing.

She suddenly said, "Girl, you even hear me? Eating that damn chicken like you haven't eaten in years and shit." They laughed again.

Swallowing, Amanda replied, "Shoo, I'm just trying not to get my head bit off!"

Smiling apologetically, Gwendolyn said, "Girl, I was hot."

Taking on a serious note, Amanda said, "And you have every right to be. I do not know why they put underqualified people in positions of power. It's ridiculous and disaster-prone." It was Gwendolyn's time to remain silent and nod. "Therefore, it's time for a change. Ya know, the Time's Up movement isn't limited to sexual harassment in the workplace, but includes discrimination and putting dumbasses in power!" They said the last part in unison, as it was a recurring theme for them.

"You shouldn't have to address the board," Amanda continued, "they should be addressing *you*."

"Thanks, girlfriend."

Amanda shook her head in disbelief at the structural power of Corporate America. Unlike Gwendolyn, Amanda was the president of her own company, so she didn't have to put up with the headaches of bosses. But she remembered the times she'd had to vividly.

"The chairman of the board asked me out to lunch," Gwendolyn confided. Amanda dropped a chicken bone in the paper bag, and her eyes widened. "When?"

"Earlier."

"Today?" Amanda asked.

"No, yesterday."

"And?"

"I told him no."

"But you wish you hadn't?"

"Naw, well, yeah, because I could address my complaint directly to him, but I didn't care to find out whether or not his intentions were on the up and up. You know, all men seem to want is sex. A simple outing may only be to prime you for the sex that they believe is inevitable. They must watch *Maury* where silly little girls give up their prize possessions for a Happy Meal," Gwendolyn said, with attitude. "The silly shit hos do reflects on us women."

"Did he come off like he was trying you?" Amanda asked seriously.

She thought about it for a moment. "No, he was more so apologetic." Amanda raised her brows. "He was kind of condescending the other day in the office, and a male chauvinist type over the phone," Gwendolyn said defensively.

"Why didn't you accept?"

"I wasn't about to go on a date with him and end up hash-tagging 'metoo.'"

"I meant accept his apology."

Gwendolyn did not respond.

"We don't compromise being a woman by accepting an apology from a man who has done us wrong," Amanda said. "That's not what being human is all about."

Feeling scolded, Gwendolyn meekly nodded her understanding.

"Honestly, I think you knew boss man was interested in you and you got scared and bolted," Amanda said, giving her an accusing eye.

"Nuh-uh, chile."

"Uh-huh," Amanda shot back with a grin. "Knowing you and that overactive brain of yours, he was jumping your bones after the second bite of his lunch," she teased.

"Naw, you got me confused, sister girl," Gwendolyn said.

"Only one confused is you," Amanda countered. "Who mistakes an apologetic invitation to lunch for an invitation to hunch?"

"I think you are the one with the overactive mind. In fact, your shit seems to be on overdrive," Gwendolyn said, good-naturedly.

"Mmm-hm," Amanda hummed with a smirk. "But you see what I see."

Gwendolyn smiled, shaking her head.

"Is he fine?" Amanda asked.

"You seen him before." Octave was on the news and in newspapers when he inherited his grandfather's company.

"I did, but I want to know what you think," Amanda said, smiling mischievously.

"I am not going there," she said dismissively.

"Asked and answered," Amanda said.

"Whatever," Gwendolyn said. But *did* she think he was fine? He did make a suit look good. And he had rugged good looks with sexy bedroom eyes. It was funny how she never noticed this when she'd seen him. A man looks were the last thing she considered.

But in Mr. Royal's case, he *was* fine. She had to give him that.

"Go on and take me back to my office," Gwendolyn said.

"Why, so you can be alone with your thoughts?"

"No, because you're being mannish." They fell into laughter.

"Ya better make him say your name," Amanda said. "Your full name."

Chapter 17

Pre-Civil-War America
Kansas Territory

"Keep a'movin'," Harriet said to the men, women, and their young'uns behind her as she chopped at high grass and weeds.

Everybody kept pace, sweating but shivering in the night. They were sweating from the strenuous journey and shivering from the fear of capture, not the cool night air. They moved with a stiff determination—not for the grueling flight but for the years of moral and physical abuse.

The abuse was mainly the results of forced labor, working for too many hours under back-breaking circumstances. When the rain came, it beat their heads and blurred their vision, hindering their work and causing frustration and apprehension. A poor job performance would be cause for a missed meal or, worse ,a whipping. That cracker took a piece of a man's spirit every time it encountered his flesh.

Harriet, holding a .38 revolver at her side, stopped and turned around to take count of her passengers. She had a fifth-grade education and a sage's instincts, so she counted by faces, not bodies. She felt responsible for their safety. In the past, slave masters had caught wind of her Underground Railroad and commissioned some of their bootlicking slaves to infiltrate her "carriage" in order to disrupt their escape and punish her for her audacity to be free and her assistance in freeing other slaves.

The slave masters did not think Harriet's plot was to free her kinsman but rather some rival plantation owner trying to steal their slaves. This made sense to a businessman trying to thrive in the business. But an ex-slave stealing slaves just to set them free was unfathomable.

Satisfied with the count, Harriet said again, "Keep a'movin'." Then she turned back around, stowing her firearm in a makeshift bag hanging at her hip. Its strap was draped over her right shoulder, crossing her torso.

She walked alongside them now. She watched them out the corner of her eye as they shuffled in a sad, stooped-over march. A depressing sight. She shook her head slowly, then nodded at the thought that one day soon they would be walking upright, chattering and smiling and laughing. And Harriet was determined to see that day.

They walked in silence, swiping at high grass and tree branches, which made too much noise. The woods seemed to be telling on them. The rustling and cracking of dry leaves and broken branches were like many voices, call out to the crackers: "Here they are! Come get 'em!" Every move they made seemed to be a step forward and backward. One step called for freedom; the other step shouted for capture. The whole scenario was frightening. The fear was at times so overbearing that one of the passengers would develop cold feet and want to head back, like a woman named Ethel a few miles back.

"I can't do this," Ethel cried. "I'm going back" Everybody turned to look at Ethel, her Black face shining with fright. Some of them looked at her with suspicion. "I'm not gonna tell master nothing," she declared. No one said anything in response.

That was when Harriet walked up to Ethel. "Come with me, chile." Harriet took Ethel out behind a tree that was out of sight and earshot of the rest of the passengers. Alone. Harriet grabbed Ethel by the shoulder with one hand and held her pistol to Ethel's face with the other.

Ethel did not see Harriet reach for the gun. It seemed to her to have materialized out of nowhere, which was just as scary as it being pointed in her face.

"Ethel, girl," Harriet began in a whisper. "Ain't no turning back for any of us. Ya can either die here or continue on and die free. Which is it?"

Ethel peered in Harriet's deep chocolate-brown eyes and registered the seriousness in them. She knew Harriet meant to kill her if she did not keep going.

"Okay," she said.

"Okay, what?" Harriet asked her, cocking the gun.

Ethel watched in horror as the cylinder on the revolver moved and the piercing bullets that looked like half of a snake's eyes peered at her, ready to strike, hoping she answered wrong.

"I'sa keep goin'," she said, after a pause. Her current fear overrode her previous fear.

Harriet placed her thumb over the pistol's hammer and slowly lowered it back in place. "Good choice," she said, but she still held the gun in Ethel's face.

After a moment, she dropped her arm, holding the gun at her thigh. She watched Ethel pensively. Ethel's eyes filled with tears, but by some mysterious force, no drop fell out. Though she was scared, she still managed to conjure up a fearless strength within.

Harriet nodded and said, "Ethel, I know what ya thinkin', and it is going to be hard not being a slave. Master telling you when to sleep and when to eat, but you knowing always you go to work or else.

"To finally make you own decisions going to be something, but I promise ya, Ethel, that something going to be great." Ethel nodded, feeling a little disarmed after Harriet's eyes changed from menacing to caring as she spoke. "And Ethel, it's still going to be hell for us as a people and as a woman. So, girl, ya got to step up and be a woman. We will be all right as long as there is—not strong women—but women period. We got our weaknesses and strengths, but we blend them and endure them as they come.

"So, I am not about to go calling a woman strong because that forces a woman to display a toughness that would cause them to hide their feelings. But our feelings are what make us fight. Whether in hurt or in love, we make it happen, ya hear me?"

"Yes, ma'am," Ethel said.

"Well, thank ya, ma'am," Harriet replied, sounding flattered. Ethel was confused by Harriet's response. "I'sa been reading the dictionary."

Ethel's eyes widened at this. Reading was a sure way to meet a cracker in the worse way back at the plantation.

"Yes, I'sa know how to read," she confirmed in a prideful yet defiant tone. "And what the dictionary defined a woman as was belonging to a category as by birth, residence, membership, or occupation. Basically, a lady, which is a woman of distinction and character," Harriet told her. "So, calling a woman *ma'am* say all that."

A soaring wave of feeling flowed to Ethel's heart. Suddnely, she felt like somebody. For the first time in fifteen years of her adult life, she felt like a *woman*.

Ethel and Harriet joined the others, and they continued to travel in tense silence through swamps and forests up through Freedom's trail—a trail that felt like hell in the process of passage to Heaven. They were on their way to meet an open field that stretched for miles, exposing them. This was dangerous land to cross. The land itself was of no danger; it was the possibility of being spotted which was where the danger lay.

Sure enough, as they trekked across the field, a caravan of white cowboys was traveling the dirt road, roughly a hundred yards off. Their lamps and torches appeared as floating lights, hovering about menacing silhouettes. The thundering footsteps of the horses they rode made them seem closer than they were.

The passengers were horrified. Ethel's heart was thumping so hard she could not help imagining it as a blood-stained fist, pounding at her chest like a door, yelling, "LET ME OUTTA HERE!" Nonetheless, she knew she had to stand her ground. Harriet's talk did not subdue the fear but enabled her to stand up to it.

Harriet looked into the distance, then turned to the horrid faces of her passengers. This was the moment where a traitor could be successful in compromising the Underground Railroad. She tightened her grip on the pistol, wishing a traitor would try. She planned to shoot him dead and hoped the shots shocked the caravan enough to make their escape. Harriet, staring an unsettling glare at her passengers, did not notice any jittering or fidgeting, the tell-tale signs of someone getting ready to haul ass.

She turned away and peered out toward the travelers to assess their situation. From what she could see, the cowboys were not too far. All it would take was a good eye to make out her and the runaway slaves, converting the caravan to a posse. They were sure to be caught and hanged in front of their people as warning for any other would-be deserters.

It was too late to order her passengers to break out and run back toward the swamps, to the cover of the forest trees and stinky, high grass. They were bound to be spotted and subsequently chased down. She could see the crackers now with their whips lashing out at the passengers, striking them down as the leather split their backs. No, she could not have that. She had to think of something else.

She frantically looked from her passengers to the cowboys until she spotted Jenks. Jenks was Roger Jenkins, an elderly Black man—or he appeared to be elderly from his years of plantation labor that had broken him down, causing him to walk with the assistance of a cane.

"Jenks, let me getcha cane," she said, as she briskly walked toward him. Jenks handed it to her. "Now I want all ya'll to get down on yo hands and knees." Frightened, and now confused, they complied and dropped down to the grass.

Harriet bowed her head in a prayer fashion, then lifted it and commanded them, "Crawl for freedom." The men, women, and children crawled for their freedom—for their lives. Without any more prompting, they scurried. Harriet stepped to the side and raised the cane in her right hand above her head with an outstretched arm.

When her passengers crept away, she followed them, waving the cane in the air. The cowboys in the distance looked on at what appeared to be a shepherd, herding his wandering sheep back home. How true this was.

The passengers traveled on without notice. When they arrived at free land, they swore to the others they met up with that Harriet had cast a spell over them, making them invisible to the cowboys. This was one of the many great undocumented tales of Harriet "Moses" Tubman.

Chapter 18

Modern-day Miami, Florida

The day of the board meeting was upon him. Octave was nervous but determined to prevent his brother from making a disaster of their grandfather's company and taking on the CEO role in the process.

His anxiety was not so much about his brother trying to take over the company, but from the board deciding to make it a joint meeting with board members as well as stockholders. To demonstrate a division in the company's leadership was not good PR for stockholders. In fact, it was bad for business.

Octave could imagine a legion of panic-stricken investors selling their stock in fear of pending loss—or worse, a crash in the company's stock causing their current prices to plunge. This would cripple Armedia, forcing the board to consider a sale bailout to salvage themselves and abandon the sinking company. This was a nightmare that he would hate to see come true.

He arrived at the company's headquarters, where the meeting would be held that morning. HQ was not a lavish building as one would expect from a multibillion-dollar company. However, it was lavish in its historical background as the foundation of the company.

Every brand has a story that it builds on, and most of that story is built around its founders. Octave M. Royal the First was an ambitious man, who came across the five-story brownstone with aspirations to turn it into something grand. This was far-fetched for a man with only a seventh grade education; but to the man with the dream, it was possible.

He set off to work two jobs full time and one part time, stealing sleep during breaks on the commode. He knew if he slept on the toilet, he was sure to keel over and either hit his head on the wall or fall off the toilet outright, either of which would wake him. It was an improvised alarm clock. He could have asked one of his coworkers to wake him up, but that was unreliable.

If he was going to realize his dream, he had to take matters seriously and discipline himself to be self-reliant until he was able to delegate. Basically, this would be his MO until he became the boss. In this way, he managed to make enough money to purchase a small office space in the building within six months of spotting it.

He got himself a business license, but initially titled his company Octave, Inc. His first products for sale were greeting cards that he made himself out of cardboard and a small printing press that he rented. The card business became his first line of communication products. Then he bought the idea of a big, but mobile, radio that he called a "Boom Box." He patented it, then spent and borrowed on the manufacture of the boom box, and the rest was history.

This nothing-to-something story resonated with consumers and especially stockholders, which made them want to be part of such ingenuity. The underdog who wins was the popular story.

Octave the Second was in that original building his grandfather bought, riding the elevator to the top floor conference room. Entering the room, he noticed a few prominent members of the board already there. The meeting was not set until nine o'clock. He was not the only one trying to get an early start.

Or was it a universal trait of overachievers to arrive early—to be the first to catch that worm called Opportunity. As a worm, opportunity is slimy, therefore, slippery—bound to wriggle away when grabbed at. But when it is caught early, just as it slips its head out of the ground, it is simple to put your hands out and patiently allow it to crawl into your palm.

"Good morning," Octave said.

"Good morning, Mr. Chairman," they chimed. They addressed him by his official title, indicating that they were ready to get down to business.

He nodded. He was ready himself. He walked to the head of the conference table, set his briefcase on top, and sat down to await the arrival of the others.

*   *   *

Gwendolyn had been up since 6:00 a.m. She had taken a shower, pulled out her outfit and pumps to wear, and after meticulously applying her makeup, she got dressed and was out the door. On her way out, she was thinking about buying a puppy. She was tired of leaving the house alone. A lonely house, she felt, was what drew ghosts.

Yes, ghosts, she told herself, as though answering an unspoken doubt. Gwendolyn had a theory about haunted houses. She believed that ghosts were conjured up in houses by the houses themselves—not left behind by some mysterious force or a past death in the house. A house was meant to be lived in—a dwelling place. As such, the house, when left alone, desires to have its rooms occupied to some capacity, and it also likes to maintain a presence within its structures.

If empty, it wills a presence in it, and a ghost or three comes to dwell there. Then Gwendolyn thought she might be woken up in the middle of the night with the foolery—leaking faucets that she just knew she did not leave on and the eerie creaking of floors and doors. The annoying torture of the ghosts trying to run her out of her own home. But a dog would be a guarding presence, holding down the house and preventing it from being lonely.

Yeah, she was going to get a puppy—a girl. The female species took pride in their possessions and were very protective. Gwendolyn knew she would have to deal with picking up shit and wiping up piss until she could potty train it, but it would be worth it.

With a cat, all she had to do was buy a pan and put kitty litter inside and they instinctively knew what to do. But cats were lazy, narcissistic, and jittery when it came down to it. A dog, though—especially a girl dog—would know how to protect the house. She wouldn't run up a tree, but bark up it.

A bad bitch over a pussy cat was more appropriate, Gwendolyn felt. She nodded, confirming her decision to purchase a puppy as she got in her car to go to the stockholders meeting.

The time was a quarter to seven. It was only a fifteen-minute drive, but she planned on arriving early to get a decent parking spot. Then she would walk to the nearby McDonald's for breakfast before the nine o'clock meeting. Also, she wanted time to review the inquiry she had written down to be ready for when they reached the questioning stage.

Chapter 19

Nine o'clock meeting time. Everyone was in attendance. The board room was packed. The twelve members of the board and their chairman sat at the conference table at the center of the spacious room while the stockholders stood around the walls. Chairs were available, but many chose not to sit. A sign of resistance perhaps? One that said they were not there to sit down but to stand up for their investments.

The setup was like a White House press room, where reporters sat waiting to grill the president's spokesperson, but instead of a podium, there was a table. Octave glanced over at Julien, who was standing to the side, wearing another unusual suit, alongside his attorney. He inwardly smiled, thinking if Julien uses his attorney to argue for his leadership role, it would be a sure sign of weakness. The members of the board would not take to anyone posed to lead them who relies on someone else to speak up for him.

Octave knew Julien would be batted down. He quickly reverted his eyes and looked straight ahead, licking his lips to suppress a smile. A victory smile would have been a grandma smile—a smile so wide it exposed his gums. He felt it improper to flash such a smile at an important meeting. When he swallowed the urge to grin, he locked eyes with Gwendolyn, who quickly glanced away. She was standing front and center among the audience of stockholders.

He stared on, hoping to catch her eye again and give a curtly nod of greeting. He did not know she was a stockholder. There was plenty he did not know about Ms. Thompson that he would not mind getting to know.

But Gwendolyn did not want to glance back at the chairman. She was angered by her body's reaction when he licked his lips. The sexiest thing a man could do was try not to be sexy. Like the unconscious licking of lips—a heightened turn-on. The uninhibited act was a naturally seductive move.

When he looked at her, she glanced away, knowing her facial expression was bound to tell on her. *Damn.* He was not only looking at her—he was smiling at her. She could not afford to look away and be like the pussycat she thought about earlier, but she needed to be like the bad bitch and stand her ground. He gave her a nod. She nodded back, but refused to smile. She did not have any reason to smile, and she did not feel obligated to return a smile.

Octave was satisfied with her acknowledgement. "Let's get this meeting started," he said out loud. Getting right down to business was a check mark for him from her.

"I will address the board, then allow the stockholders the opportunity to address their concerns."

What about Mr. Quincy? Gwendolyn thought. Usually, the CEO of the company addressed the stockholders, not the chairman of the board.

"Mr. Quincy is currently the interim CEO, and the permanent filling of the CEO position is the topic of discussion," Octave said, answering her unasked question. "Armedia is undergoing a transition. My brother, who is a major stockholder and descendent of the founder of the company, has suggested that he would be a contender for the job."

Julien's lawyer opened his briefcase and pulled out some files. He turned and handed them to Julien and stepped back as Julien stepped forward.

"Thank you, Samuel," Julien said, then turned to his brother. "And thank you, Mr. Chairman," he told Octave, keeping up the formalities. "Ladies and gentlemen. I am Julien Royal and I wish to present a proposal along with my request for CEO. I have here," he raised the files up to shoulder height, "a presentation of the future progress of Armedia." He handed the stack to Octave.

"Mr. Chairman, if you would, please take one and pass it down." Julien waited for the papers to go around the table before continuing. "What's in your hands is the blueprint for wealth."

The board members looked down at the papers they held, waiting for an explanation. If Julien himself could not make them believers, they were sure that the papers in front of them wouldn't convince them. If the creator couldn't break down the plan, then the papers weren't going to either. And the board had no desire to breathe life into someone else's whims.

"The market for smartphones is a cult-like following. Apple and Samsung are dishing out cell phones every six months, garnering billions of dollars from each release."

"Excuse me," Gwendolyn said, raising her hand.

"Yes," Julien said.

"Can the stockholders have a copy of your presentation?"

"Sure," he said. "However, I was under the impression that I was going to address the board only, so I didn't bring additional copies. It would be time-consuming to make copies now."

"You can have mine," Octave told her, rising from his seat. Gwendolyn watched him move toward her. When, for a split second, he stood by his brother, they were mirror opposites, but dissimilar in a way that was unconsciously detected.

He handed her the papers wearing that sexy smile. "Thank you," she said and immediately peered down at the papers. It was obvious that she was the only stockholder in the audience interested in the presentation, so there was no need for her to pass it around. Assessment of products, production analysis, and the likes were her thing, so if the presentation were on point, she would know.

Octave felt like he one-upped Julien. His unpreparedness placed him one down with the stockholders, who would have a say in the matter.

"Okay," Julien said, as Octave sat back down. "We are not going to try to keep up with the Joneses in the cell phone industry. I plan to profit off the extensive apps. Application enhancements are what quantify cell phone advancements. So, I feel if we tap into developing applications, creating and selling, we could profit off of them and expand in the business. And—" He was cut off by Gwendolyn waving her hand in the air.

"Yes, miss?" Julien asked, although a part of him wished he had not.

"Well, I would have to voice the fact that I don't see the potential in this plan."

"Why is that?" he asked, only because it was expected of him.

"Applications are not safe. There have been many applications, sold to big companies like ours, that have not been completed, and some that have not been tested to see if multiple users could hold. As a result, the apps are riddled with glitches. To prevent this, the apps would have to be monitored in real time, which requires hired hands that subsequently require money.

"So, it comes to the question of cost of production. And the overhead of such a venture is flakey at best. There is no set cost and no analytical information to assist us in determining whether or not it would be cost effective. It's a possibility that we may lose more than we gain," Gwendolyn concluded.

Julien wondered if she was a plant from his brother to thwart his pursuit of the CEO seat. "And you are, who?" he asked, as if she would voluntarily admit that she was planted by his brother.

"I am a concerned investor at the moment, sir," she replied.

The stockholders grunted and hummed their agreement, inadvertently placing her as the leader of the group. And why wouldn't they, when the woman evidently knew what she was talking about?

"I see," Julien said. "But I assure you there's nothing to be concerned about. If we stay in the race, we would be relevant, and hence, profit from our competitiveness."

"With all due respect, sir, I cannot compute competitiveness as profitable. I can only see ousting competitors or blowing past them as profitable," Gwendolyn countered, followed by the agreeable chuckles of her fellow investors.

Octave looked on with pride. He was proud of her for taking a stance and safeguarding her investment. He looked up at his brother, whose mouth was wide open. He was clearly convinced that Gwendolyn was the human version of a monkey wrench that he most likely thought Octave threw at him to sabotage his plans.

Julien waited a moment, finally closing his mouth as he thought about what he was going to say. "I understand, ma'am. But we are equipped to do just that." Gwendolyn stayed silent. "Is it not a counter game we play?"

She just stared at him, knowing he did not know what the hell he was talking about but was trying to use her to make his case. She knew this game well from working under Mr. Trent.

"I know you are a woman who knows her business and that you would agree that it's tit for tat in marketing," Julien said, motioning his hand in her direction for emphasis.

Gwendolyn frowned, realizing her silence served the same purpose. She was conscious of the leadership role she had been given by the stockholders, who seemed fine with letting her argue for them. She did not want to let them or herself down because this guy was not fit for the CEO position.

"That *is* my business," she said, "and I know that any product can be marketed, but not all can be profitable, and some are not even worth the time.

"I mean, the application market can be tapped into, but it's not a solid market and surely not one that could be utilized to sustain the company, nor is it the ultimate key to the company's growth."

"This is just one project that I am presenting," Julien defended. "There will be more to come soon. But innovation would be the motto of Armedia. Because innovation is the key to successful businesses like ours."

Gwendolyn had to admit that what he said sounded good, even the stockholders were swayed by his words. But she knew the whole "innovation is success" was a sure seller because it was preached so much that it was considered truth.

Semantics was not mathematics. Fifty words of assurance did not produce numbers as in dividends for investors. "That sounds good, sir. But as we all can recall, it was innovation that sold Samsung phones that burn down houses and nearly crash airplanes. How's that for innovation as success?"

"That is a good argument, ma'am. However, I am not here to argue facts. My main objective in this presentation is to show my willingness to take a step forward," Julien said. "The blows that were taken by Samsung led them to an unfortunate spot.

"Our stake in the whole equation is that Apple and Samsung took on a billion dollars in sales, and our applications would take at least twenty percent of that, which would garner the company hundreds of millions of dollars amid glitches and all," Julien said, well put.

Octave was surprised at his brother's response. It was obvious that Julien had done his homework. This was not what he had anticipated from him, but he did anticipate a fight, so he was prepared for that.

"Furthermore," Julien continued, "We are currently in production of numerous devices that are within our means. Our marketing and sales execs have summarized a—um, what I would call an itinerary of products and projected sales that would keep us in the game for years to come."

A summary of projections? Octave thought. This was supposed to be his ace in the hole to prove Julien was unfit for the CEO position. How in the hell did he get this information?

"I am familiar with the projections," Gwendolyn said. "Nonetheless, a projection is mere theory. What I would like to know is how as CEO do you plan on executing those predicted sales?"

Julien felt the woman was fishing, that she was not aware of such projections and was simply testing him. She most definitely had to be in cahoots with his brother.

"Ma'am, how is it that you are privy to such information?" he asked, intending to expose her and charge his brother with insider trading, which was in an attempt to prevent him from being CEO and taking his brother's chair out of mere jealousy and sibling rivalry. But he was unprepared for her response.

"I am the one who projected them," she said. The board members snapped their necks to look at her, and the stockholders gasped.

Octave smiled. He had been wrong. If Julien had done his homework, he would have visited the sales and marketing department and run into Mr. Trent who would have introduced him to Ms. Thompson. This took Julien two down.

"Ms. Thompson, would you mind introducing yourself, please?" Octave said.

"Yes, I am Gwendolyn Thompson, employee of Armedia at sales and marketing."

Julien turned to his brother. "You knew who she was all along, so you planted her here to make me look bad?" he accused.

"Yes, I knew of her employment, but I had no idea she was a stockholder—um, concerned investor, I mean. In fact, it's a surprising pleasure to have someone of keen knowledge here as an asset to the company and an investor," Octave told him.

"Pleasure" was all Gwendolyn heard him say. She pushed it to the back of her head and said, "My concern as an investor is the management at

Armedia." There, she said it. It may not get her the CEO spot, but at least she could try to change how things were ran. That was her next best reason for exposing her expertise in management. She refused to be a hidden figure.

"And what's wrong with the management of our company, Ms. Thompson?" Octave asked.

"Well, for one, the micromanaging chain of command is improperly in place. Duties are being neglected, and skilled employees are not being acknowledged nor compensated, which are ingredients for chaos that has no method or organization to produce the necessary results."

Then she turned to Julien. "My question to you, Mr. Royal, is how as the CEO of the company would you handle this chaotic management that is sure to affect the very same sale projections you spoke of?"

"I hear your grievance," Julien said. "But you can rest assured that Armedia would be under a new and improved management."

"Thanks for clearing that up, sir," Gwendolyn said with sarcasm, which was detected by the attendants. Octave could not wait to hear Julien's response.

"I'm glad I was able to clarify for you," he said. *Whoa!* Octave could not believe how boldly Julien dismissed Ms. Thomson's sarcasm.

"No, you didn't clarify anything, sir. I was being sarcastic."

"And I wasn't," he said tersely. Then he turned to Octave and asked, "Shall we proceed with the board's recommendation?"

Octave looked at Gwendolyn and watched how she bit her tongue with an unnatural effort. "Would the stockholders like to respond?"

Gwendolyn took a deep breath and said, "I am against the appointment of a CEO who uses semantics instead of facts to outline a situation in important matters as these." She shook her head sadly. "This is not politics, this is business. Show *then* Tell is our game. Not Tell for Show. And if my word means nothing as a stockholder, then I don't need to hold any stock."

Cheers and applause broke out from the stockholders. "Let's have a little order in here, please," Octave announced. When everyone calmed down, he said, "Let's recess for an hour and then get back to more pressing topics." It was not late, but the lunch hour was approaching.

Julien's attorney grabbed his briefcase off the table, and he and Julien set off to regroup. Everyone else piled up at the door to leave the room.

Octave kept his eyes on Gwendolyn, wanting to get her opinion on what he sought to do today. Surely, she had proven herself insightful.

He stood up and was striding to the door to catch her when Valencia Scott, CEO of Home Depot and Armedia board member said, "Mr. Chairman, may I speak to you please?" Octave looked at her and tried to suppress his annoyance, but he knew he hadn't because when he paused, she said, "I'm sorry to bother you, but I have an eleven o'clock with a few independent builders at our local branch department stores that I really need to contract. So, I can't stay too long."

Valencia's vote for him was a sure thing when he announced his desire to take the CEO position. They had a brief fling and set things off out of mutual respect. The sophisticated, thick, chocolate woman was a Milky Way—as sweet inside as the delicious candy.

"I see," he said, but only saw her as a vote that was leaving. He looked at his watch. It was a quarter to eleven. "Is it possible for you to head off and be back within the hour?"

"I doubt it," she said. "These are independent contractors that I must see individually." Octave could understand her plight. If she had all of them in one room, it would be a price war, with somebody being disappointed or paying out too much for different services at once.

"All right, we'll make do without you."

"Okay, sorry," she said, rising up on her toes and kissing him on the cheek. "Just fill me in later. But I can tell you now, I don't see myself voting for your twin." Octave frantically looked around to see who saw Valencia kiss him—mainly he checked for Gwendolyn, who must have left already.

Satisfied, he said, "What about me?"

Valencia made a backward duck move with her neck. "You? As in, you as CEO of Armedia?" she asked incredulously.

"Yes, me. Something wrong with that?"

"No. I just didn't think you would be interested in the position, that's all. But," she shrugged, "if you are interested, I think you would be a good candidate. You got my vote."

Octave nodded, "Thanks, Valencia."

"It isn't a thing," she said. "Let me go now."

"All right, bye."

Valencia headed off and he followed, hoping to find Gwendolyn for a chat, to possibly win her to his side.

He spotted Gwendolyn in the hall and scurried to catch up to her as she headed out. The stockholders were commending her, literally patting her on her back for her performance and courage. They called her by name, and all wanted to know about and be involved in only investments that were Gwendolyn Thompson approved.

Chapter 20

Turn of the Twentieth Century American Midwest

Tired of busting her ass and getting no pay, Sarah McWilliams wanted more. More money and more prestige, but less struggling to make ends meet. Hard times, she felt, defined being Black and female, but she was determined to make life easier for herself and those around her.

There was a dream in America that she had overheard in Mr. and Mrs. Harris's house one day when she was cleaning up. Mr. Harris was a middle-aged white man, who was trying to make a point to his young white wife about why he spent money so freely.

"In America, we can live like kings and queens—at least aristocrats," Mr. Harris said. "It's the 'American Dream' to live lavishly."

The American Dream is to live lavish, Sarah thought. Those words resonated with her. Slavery had been over for decades, but she and her kind were still enduring slavish labor to make ends meet. Were they not Americans to live lavish, not slavish? She was in her own house now, thinking about how it was that she would make it happen.

Her house was a run-down shack, surrounded by mud and dead grass. She hated living there as much as she hated living as broke as her shack house. Sarah was broke financially but rich in pride. She kept herself up in clean clothes and would concoct all types of experimental hair products to keep her hair rich and shining. Because, like any woman, she was vain about her appearance. With the American Dream in mind, an idea about how to get a little extra money leapt up like one of the frogs that patrolled her yard.

She could take her hair product on the road, appealing to the vanity of her species. Helping them would help her. She hurried to the kitchen.

Sarah had been wrestling through the night, mixing substances together, trying to concoct an even grander product than the one she had been using. She sliced potatoes, added stinking lye, as well as some cherries she picked off the bushes along the dirt road that bordered her house. Sarah created different formulas and tested them all on herself.

Some formulas hit right on, one or two nearly caused her to lose a whole mane of hair, and all of them were the stinkiest. She had to come up with a formula that worked well and smelled decent.

The next day, after working through the night, she went to town and purchased some incense and picked more cherries. She wanted to blend the two products to come up with a pleasant scent. But she also didn't want women use her product on a picnic date and lie down and become a meal for ants. So she had to somehow strain the cherries' flavor and keep the cherry scent. But how?

She decided to smash up the cherries to squeeze out their juice into a bowl. Using a strainer, she poured the juice into a pot, then threw in the incense and mixed in her formula to boil together. She hovered over a big pot that sat on a roaring fire with her hair a mess from experimenting on herself with her own product.

Sweat dripped from her forehead and down the sides of her face, missing her wide, intensely focused eyes. She looked like a witch cooking up a potion. Finished. She poured the formula into a wooden bowl to cool. She would let it sit there until the morning, when she would try it out.

Chapter 21

Morning came, a mere couple of hours after she finished. The formula was cool, but now she had to test it. Sarah rose out of her bed, bouncing on the springy mattress in the process, and went to the kitchen. There, she stood over the bowl that sat on a makeshift dining table—a tabletop supported by old wooden crates.

Sarah dipped her nose over the bowl and took a whiff. "Mmmm," she murmured. The cherry incense scent was pleasant. She nodded and freshened up, using the new batch of hair formula.

Drying her hair in front of the mirror over her bathroom sink, Sarah felt its soft but strong texture. And the room was filled with a sweet aroma that she knew came from her product. The sweet perfume made her feel even fresher than the actual bathing.

"Yes, SIR!" she exclaimed, knowing she had a hit.

She fluffed her hair and blinked her red eyes. Some of the formula had gotten into her eyes, causing them to burn. She made a note to place a warning on the jars for users to keep it out of their eyes, to not swallow it, and to keep it out of reach of kids. She could imagine a young'un mistaking the sweet cherry scent for actual candy and consuming it. The very thought of such made her cross herself.

Sarah dressed, filled up a crate with her hair product and stowed it in a wagon, then headed out to make her first sale. At first, she thought about giving women a sample of the product with information on where they could purchase their own bottle, but then she thought against it. She was in it to win it. Why underplay her product? It was more appealing to consumers that the product was ready for use. And if they did not like it, they could seek a refund or never buy from her again.

She talked to everybody she knew, giving them her sales pitch. She approached women on the streets and men who had women in their lives—whether they were their wives or mamas. She told them all about her new fabulously sweet product that wasn't whitey's typical shampoo. It was a Black woman's "glampoo, chile boo!" She proclaimed to all. And it worked. Sarah sold every jar she had.

On her way home, she purchased more incense and paid some local kids a dime to pick as many cherries as possible. Back in her kitchen, she brewed another batch. In the process, she wrote down the ingredients, though she knew them by heart. This was an instinct that paid off as her business bloomed and she had to patent her product and hire other women to use their kitchens to help her manufacture it.

Business was lovely for Sarah. She bought a fabulous stagecoach and hired a chauffeur to drive her on her sales routes and to her meetings with department store owners to negotiate a contract to place her products on their shelves. She bought a house—a beautiful brick house that sat on the edge of a valley that was bursting with daffodils and hyacinths. And when the rainbows glowed in the sky, they seemed to come from the flowers and end at her house, where she lived and stored her gold mine.

She was booming, with sell reps traveling all over the state and abroad, selling her products for a nice commission. And they were selling out everywhere. Although she set out to appeal to women of color, her hair product sold to all women, and this made her a very rich woman.

Within a few years of production, she made her first million dollars. This made her the first self-made woman millionaire in the world. When news of Sarah's newfound fortune leaked out, she started receiving invitations to prestigious parties and events.

She was rich and living the American dream. Sarah was smiling a lot lately; she had gone from being too tired to smile and not having anything worth smiling about to smiling up a storm. She was happy with her fortune and the prestige that came with it. From this happy feeling and high status, she gave herself the distinguished moniker Madam C. J. Walker.

Chapter 22

Life was good for "the Madam," which was what people came to call her. She found herself traveling to cities and socializing with powerful people of all races, even venturing inside political circles. It was a wonder how in a racially divided time that abundance of money made skin color the same, or at least neutral.

However, the Madam found herself thwarted from expanding her wealth by frivolous taxes.

At a fundraiser party for a congressman in New York City, she inquired about the "tax invasion" (what she dubbed her dilemma) to a mysterious, short white man with a long nose. He had approached her earlier, out the blue as if he materialized at her side like some type of magic elf.

"Hello, Madam." He greeted her with a smile that did not reach his inquisitive eyes.

"Hi ya do, sir," she responded. She wondered whether he knew her by name or called all ladies of importance *madam*.

"Nice party," he said in a soft-spoken manner.

"No, but if you say." She shrugged.

He chuckled. "I am just saying," he said and a little of his New York City accent seeped out. "These events are necessary to fulfill quotas and such," he added.

She looked at him up and down, taking him in. He wore a tailored black suit with a silky white dress shirt and custom silver ML cufflinks. *He must be a political man,* she thought. *Maybe he knows a thing or two about the tax invasion.*

"Excuse me, sir," she began. "I am unfamiliar with these settings, but I am aware of the government figures imposing taxes. But I am lost on why, and especially how. What that be about?"

He smiled again, revealing fine, even, white teeth that the Madam was sure were the work of a professional instead of Mother Nature.

"I am glad you asked, Madam."

She nodded. Not from his response but from receiving the answer to her earlier question. He did know her by name.

"These political people could be helpful to your establishment," he told her, revealing to her that he also knew about her business, which was not surprising since she had been featured in almost every syndicated press across the country. "You've been indirectly contributing to these figures, but you aren't being compensated for it."

She raised her brows as if to say, "Go on."

"My friends and I placed these figures in office to delegate and regulate our business endeavors. And we have been paying attention to you," he confided. "We have concluded that you could be a major player in an inevitable movement."

"What inevitable movement?" she asked.

"The women's right to vote," he said. "Suffrage is what makes and breaks these political figures. And with your Booker-T.-Washington, pull-yourself-up-by-the-bootstraps, independent attitude, you are the perfect contender to lead this movement and propel it."

He paused to let his words to sink in. "This movement could lead to other rights for women in America and eventually around the world," he said.

This all sounded good to her, and God knew she knew a thing or two about the unfairness foisted upon the female species, but her best interest was not piqued.

After reading the disinterest and skepticism on her face, he said, "And when you've gathered the right to vote, you control the very people who control the taxes, solving your current problem."

Now *that* was interesting. "Where do I begin?" she asked.

The little man smiled.

*　　*　　*

Weeks after, the Madam formed a coalition with other women, lending her voice and prestige to the movement. The women came out of the woodwork like an army of ants in summer. They met in houses at first, then schools, and eventually arenas. They had their mottos, slogans, and the likes to breathe life into such a movement.

The Madam gave a memorable speech at a packed arena: "Women, woman, girlfriend—it is not fit for nature to take on a common ground." Standing on stage behind a podium, she turned her head, scanning the audience.

"Some grounds build rock that molds over, while some grounds produce the loveliest flowers the world has ever seen. The ground we produce may be hard and moldy, or beautiful and soft. The meaning of 'go hard or go home' does not qualify for us. Our homes are not home. They are a prison of sorts when it is assumed that we have to be there twenty-four-seven. Slaving for no pay, and we sho'nuff don't have any say. But we ain't having it."

The crowd of women roared with cheers and claps. When the crowd subsided, and after a swig of water from the glass she kept on the podium, the Madam continued: "We are not having it. We are not doormats. We are not third-class citizens of this country. We are not slaves. Slavery passed, racism is at a minimum, but the woman is still enslaved and discriminated against. We—are—not—having—it!" The Madam chopped the air with her hand after every word.

The crowd repeated. "WE ARE NOT HAVING IT!"

"We are woman?"

"WE ARE WOMAN!"

This was one of several empowering speeches the Madam made. She even took on the political scene, rallying voters to exercise their right to vote and effect change. The little guy, who she found out was the Jewish gangster Meyer Lansky, was right. But he did not tell her about the empowerment such a movement would inspire. In 1920, women got the vote, and a big reason for it was thanks to extraordinary women making an extraordinary effort. These women were the movement.

Who would have thought that a woman who once scrubbed floors for others, practically a slave, would be at the forefront of this movement? Madam C. J. Walker was a pioneer who inspired generations of women in years to come. Oprah Winfrey, who surpassed her by becoming the world's first self-made woman billionaire, contributed her achievement to the Madam's example and became the Madam of modern times.

Madam C. J. Walker's legacy became women's legacy. There are plenty of self-made women now, but Madam C. J. Walker's name would be forever associated with women in power.

Chapter 23

Modern-day Miami, Florida

The feeling of empowerment coursed through her veins and filled up her brain. Gwendolyn was an intelligent woman, who was very good at what she did. But to be able to stick her neck out and dare anybody to chop it off was badass.

The CEO position was boss, but she would be chief of someone else's tribe. That would make her the leader of a pack controlled by another, which did not sit well with her now, as she sat in the McDonald's with a whole bunch of strangers. They looked at her as a force to be reckoned with, which coincided with how she was feeling.

But suddenly, her CEO goal was not all that appealing. An investment firm seemed to be in demand. The thought of starting an investment company came when a man walked up and introduced himself.

"Hello, I'm Lensey Haskins," he said, putting out his hand.

"Gwendolyn Thompson," she said, taking his hand.

"Don't I know it," he told her. "Your name rings bells around here like a Las Vegas slot machine." She laughed.

Lensey was a tall, light skinned man with a smooth bald head and an evenly trimmed beard. Judging by his looks and accent, she could tell he was from an island in the Caribbean. He wore a suit of his own device, a color and style all his own. Surprisingly, he did not look like a clown, but seemed to personify his suit. The outfit made a statement: *I am a man with character, humor, and love.*

"You are too much," she said.

"No, you are," he replied. "With that in mind, I was wondering, are you investing in anything else?"

"Yes. In my business, I follow a lot of companies. Investing was inevitable."

He dug in his pocket and came out with a card. "You can sign me up as a client," he told her, handing her the card. "I'm looking to expand my wealth. I know with you my money's in good hands."

The thought of starting an investment firm did not seem too bad. *But would it be prosperous?* That was an odd question after telling Lensey her business. She had no reason to doubt herself. Without a doubt, she could run a successful investment firm.

Fuck it, she thought to herself. She was going to do it. She had always known she had boss potential, so why wait for a bucket of kitty litter when she was in the habit of relieving herself when the door was open.

She grabbed the cup of McCafé that sat in front of her and took a sip, smiling to herself and nodding. *An investment firm it is*, she thought just as she felt a tap on her shoulder. Turning toward the tap caused her smile to disappear.

"Excuse me, Ms. Thompson," Octave said. "May I speak to you for a moment, please?"

Embarrassed by her rude reaction to the shock of his presence, she stuttered, "Um, sure."

"Alone," he said, smiling at the other occupants at the table in apology.

She nodded. "Of course. Excuse me, ya'll," she said as she scooted out of the booth.

Gwendolyn and Octave walked to a counter on the other side of the restaurant. Octave stood on guard as she sat on the stool, then he sat beside her. She set her cup on the counter and looked at him attentively.

"Thanks for seeing me," he said, and she nodded, curious. "I admired you at the meeting."

Admired me? Gwendolyn thought that was an odd choice of words to praise a board meeting performance, but maybe she was reading too much into it. She had to admit, she found the man attractive. She could hear Amanda now at such an admission. "Ease up, Stella G.," she would exclaim, and "Catch yo' gruuuve baack," in a poor Shaggy impersonation. She smiled at this thought, and he smiled back.

Whoa, wrong signal. She erased her smile and said, "Thank you."

"As you saw," he said, skipping to the point, "My brother is set on ruining the company." She noted how he used the word *ruining* in place of *running*. "And I can't allow that. It's clear he is going to be persistent in the matter. I don't know where he got the idea to be CEO."

She could but kept it to herself. Octave, obviously frustrated, talked on about the nerve and arrogance of his brother.

She once thought Octave was arrogant and brazen, but after encountering his twin, she realized he was the opposite. He explained to her his theory on his brother's reason for wanting to run their grandfather's company as being derived from sibling rivalry. It was an opposition that went back as far as when they were toddlers; they realized then that they weren't two of the same people, but individuals that looked a lot alike. It was like looking in a mirror and seeing yourself, but then realizing that the reflection was not you.

Gwendolyn laughed at that. She could imagine two little boys looking in anger and disappointment at one another, thinking, *You are not me, but you look like me. You should be like me!*

That was funny, but she tried not to laugh too much and offend him. She could see that he was annoyed by his brother, and she did not want to rile him up anymore. He went on to stress how his grandfather made a stipulation in his will. Only one of them could earn the right to run his company. Then he told her how he'd put himself through college, earned a master's in business, and found out everything he could about his grandfather's business.

"I learned the most," he said, "from the analysis report generated by Mr. Trent on sales and marketing."

"What was that?" she asked. "Mr. Trent's what?"

"I thought I could learn more about my grandfather's business by studying its sales, so I got a copy of Mr. Trent's sales and marketing analysis," he explained. She frowned. "That was my whole reason for visiting him the other day—to show my appreciation. I was planning to promote him to chief marketing officer and raising his pay."

She paused to collect herself. If she claimed to be the author of every sales and marketing document, she would be whining. He would see her as weak and call her every derogatory term for a woman in a so-called man's world.

She took a deep breath, then leveled her eyes to his. "Mr. Royal, the very information that garnered you your inheritance was authored by me." There, she said it in an even tone with no attitude. She simply stated a fact.

"You did?" he asked. "I assumed it was Mr. Trent since he gave it to me. I didn't know."

"Nobody knows the ghostwriters until their spirits get restless and they decide not to be an apparition anymore, but to stand solid in their aspiration to write."

"Well, I could make you CMO! God knows you deserve it," he said. "And Mr. Trent could work for you or find some other work."

"Huh? Trent work? I'd love to see that," she said. "Look, I appreciate your acknowledgement. I really do. Being recognized for your deeds when due is an honor. But I am turning in my resignation."

"What?" he asked in surprise. "Why?"

"Today I got a chance to take control like a boss," she said as humbly as possible, but she really wanted to say it like Janet. "And I liked it. That's not all. A window of opportunity was opened for me today that I plan to take advantage of by starting my own investment company."

"I see," he said. "Would you mind consulting Armedia on sales and marketing?"

Consulting Armedia? That was another business venture to explore, she thought. She would be in demand on all levels. There was no law against investing in a company you consulted for.

"Sure, I could do that," she said. He nodded.

Gwendolyn appreciated him for that. When she disclosed her plan to go into business for herself, he did not scrunch his face in doubt or proclaim how rash her idea was. He just heard her out and took her word for it, even offering her business, which meant he was confident that she could pull it all off. Basically, he believed in her like she did herself. That really touched her.

"Well, since you are no longer going to be employed at Armedia, do you mind having dinner with me?"

"Technically, I still work there," she said, "so is this sexual harassment on the job?"

"Only if I try to force you out on a date with subtle threats of job security. And be an asshole in the process," he responded with a smirk.

"Well then, I guess I will accept your offer," she said, grinning.

"You made it sound like a business agreement."

"It is," she told him. He gave her a look like that was not what he had in mind. "Personal business," she added. "We are officially going out on a personal date."

He smiled in relief, and she smiled back in relief. She was finally going to do the things she wanted to do.

Chapter 24

America in the 1980s–2017
Houston, Texas

Janet moved like a robot short circuiting with a rhythm. Whoa, Janet Jackson was in control, the little girl thought as she watched her perform on television while sitting on a couch in her living room. The robotic-rhythmic dance turned into a loose puppet with Janet's mind as the puppeteer. It was amazing to watch, and even more so because she not only had awesome inhuman dance moves, but she sang to the beat as well.

"Wow!" the little girl exclaimed, then she jumped up and started imitating Janet's dance moves and singing. She was actually on beat with her feet and on key with her voice. She danced with an abandonment, oblivious to anyone. Well, not *everyone*. She had her imaginary audience cheering her on and singing along as she performed like Janet, sporting a feminine military outfit that embodied control. Boldness is a beautiful woman's signature.

As she performed unaware, her dad walked in the room, carrying a cup of coffee that he placed on a shelf next to his favorite couch. He knew the song and that it was reaching its end. The little girl stomped and ground, moving her head and arms with attitude. She came to the conclusion of the song and froze in a defiant pose, a mean mug on her face.

CLAP, CLAP, CLAP, CLAP! She spun around, her mean mug replaced with one of shock from being caught in the act.

She smiled when she saw her daddy, then put on a shy expression.

"Don't try to go in ya lil' cacoon now. I caught the way you did your thing like Janet," he told her, then held his arms out. The little girl took the cue and ran into his arms. Lifting her off the ground, he said, "You are a talented little girl."

"I know," she replied.

"And sure of yourself. You sure you not twenty-one instead of eight?" he asked with wide eyes, feigning shock.

She giggled. "I am eight, Daddy." However, she knew that one day soon, she would be performing before crowds like Janet.

"Sometimes, Bey, it's hard to tell," he said, then laughed. "Ya one of the fortunate with innate talent, sweetheart. Not everybody has that."

"Maybe that is because they don't want it like I do," she said.

He squinted an eye and tilted his head back in a questioning expression. "Well, putting it that way, you may be right."

She had known she wanted to be a performer since she could remember. It was her dream to perform worldwide for millions, touching that number of hearts and more, taking in the vibe of the crowd shouting out her name—her actual name. Some would call her Be-yoncé and Beyonce, but they would know it's Beyoncé when she made it. She really felt she was a child of fortune. Her mother and father were very supportive of her goal and encouraged her to hone her talent and build her skills.

Her dad made sure she performed in contests, and she happily contended with the desire to win. Later, when little Beyoncé became a teenager, her father became her manager and started a singing group with her homegirls from Houston called "Destiny's Child."

Beyoncé didn't know about anyone else, but she knew what she wanted. When she performed, she wanted to stir the crowd, to entertain in a way in which they would become involved as unwitting yet willing participants. Like when she was in her living room in front of the TV watching Janet perform. To inspire a little girl like Janet inspired her was the supreme performance—a performance that sparked another dreamer to see their dream fulfilled.

Everyone, she felt, could do what they wanted if they truly wanted it. Normalcy was a choice, especially in America and other democracies. Any girl could become a queen if she worked hard and extra smart. Destiny's Child went on to sell millions of records and outlasted many girl groups of the time. They were winning, like Beyonce' always set out to do.

Then the inevitable happened at the turn of the twenty-first century: They broke up. Or since they were from Texas, it could be said that they came to their "last rodeo." That was it for Destiny's Child, but Beyoncé still felt like a child of fortune, even though she was now a woman.

One night, back at her parents' house, she wanted to speak to her father. He was in his home office, sitting at his desk, playing himself in chess. Beyoncé stood at the door for a minute while he strategized about how to beat himself, then she tapped on the door and entered.

He looked up from the game and smiled at her. "Hey, baby."

"Hey, Daddy," she said.

He took her in, noticing how his little girl had blossomed. "What's up?" he asked. He could tell this wasn't a mere social call. He also knew she might be a little depressed about the group breaking up.

"Daddy, it's about the group breaking up."

He nodded, thinking he was right in his assessment. "I understand, sweetheart."

"Do you, Dad?" she asked, looking seriously into his eyes.

From her intense eye contact, he felt he probably did not. "Well, I know the group breaking up was a big heartbreak for you."

"It was," she said. "But I'm not finished, Dad. I don't feel complete. I want more." He didn't respond, so she continued. "In the group, I accomplished only a little of what I wanted to as a performer. But that accomplishment was so small that even I couldn't see it. And this I can't accept. I feel my dream is unfulfilled."

"So, you want to form another group?" he asked, although he knew she was ready to fly solo. It was her time—like Diana Ross, when she became supreme and did not need the Supremes anymore.

"I am ready to go on my own," she declared. And he smiled.

As a result of this conversation with her father/manager, she pursued an independent career. She went on to perform solo, giving memorable performance after memorable performance. Prior to her shows, she consulted with the best choreographers to come up with the meanest, dopest dance moves, and her mother designed her original outfits to dazzle the crowds.

Beyoncé's life was going in the direction she set out for it to go. She was not only known by name; she was known as a queen. She even met her king, who some thought was a god, and they became an item. Did that make her a goddess? She would not bother answering that question. Her life was all she sought it out to be…yet she still wanted more.

She told her cousin Kelly Rowland at her sister's baby shower, "I want more than what I have going on in my career."

Kelly thought, *What more could Beyoncé ask for?*

"What you? Come on, child star, you 'bout to crash the stage?"

"Naw, girl," she said. "I feel so good. I made my dream come true. I feel like Sasha Fierce, and I think every woman in the world should feel like this. To know such a feeling is in fact a reality realizable."

Kelly nodded, then shrugged. "In that case, do whatcha do."

So she, Queen Bey, set out to perform songs that not only women could relate to, but resonated with them. And she did, causing women of every walk of life, shape, size, and color to claim their rightful crown.

Nevertheless, it was not until she reclaimed her creole roots and expanded the women's empowerment movement, ordering women to get into formation, that her star rose to her expectations. That was not all. She donned an ultra-feminine, sexy military outfit and danced in that robotic-rhythmic way like Janet at the Superbowl. She was not only talking to that little girl, for her to get in step, but all women.

"OKAY, LADIES, LET'S GET IN FORMATION!" she sang, letting them know that they too were in control. And like the song, she, along with millions of women, slayed.

Chapter 25

Modern-day Miami, Florida

Gwendolyn was glad she decided to go out with Octave. He was a nice man, not to mention ambitious, cute, strong, and surprisingly sensitive. She loved how they both freely revealed to one another their hearts, getting personal, when she could tell that he, like herself, was the private type.

And Gwendolyn was excelling in her business. The day of the board/ stockholders meeting in McDonald's, she copped a dozen clients by word of mouth and a few handkerchief contracts signed for future business.

"Ms. CEO" was her new title, along with "Founder," which was even more prestigious and deserved. She had known that one day she would be boss. It was embedded in her as woman. Gwendolyn felt a womn was meant to run things—whether her household or a business, a woman was meant to rule.

Seated at a dinner table across from Octave in a secluded corner of an upscale restaurant, she felt very assertive and giddily romanced. They were in Coral Gables' CocoWalk. The setting was beautiful. The restaurant and strip had a picturesque setting that made her feel like a star in romance movie. This made her smile inwardly and think about Amanda.

"Girl, you are going to feel good—during and after," Amanda said when Gwendolyn told her Octave asked her out again and she accepted. "Especially," Amanda went on, "since you are a boss amongst bosses now. Going out with a boss man as a lady boss."

And at that moment in the restaurant, after strolling down the strip, she did feel good.

Gwendolyn found herself feeling so comfortable with him that she confided in him frequently. And he seemed comfortable with her sharing with him—not judging her, just being supportive. They conversed about personal matters of likes and dislikes, but it was inevitable that they would eventually begin to talk shop.

It was Saturday, and the rescheduled board/stockholders meeting was on Tuesday. When they returned from their lunch break, Octave informed the attendees about Valencia's abrupt departure and rescheduled the meeting.

"My brother trying to take over is a hard pill to swallow," he confided in her. She nodded but didn't really understand their sibling rivalry because she did not have any siblings. "I talked to him yesterday, and he grilled me about you."

"About me?" she said, in surprise.

"Yeah, he was sure I planted you there to thwart his plans. Then when I denied it vehemently, he sensed, the way we twins sometimes do, that I was telling the truth," Octave said. "But then he started talking about how sexy you were—holding your ground, not being fussy or irritable, but self-assured and matter-of-fact and…beautiful."

She squinted at the compliment.

"And you know what?" he continued. "For the first time in years, I agreed with my brother."

Gwendolyn's eyes widened, then she smiled. Her cheeks were hot from blushing. She felt Julien's compliment was the typical sexist retort and inappropriate, but when Octave said he agreed, it felt sincere and appropriate. "Thank you," she said.

He smiled, happy to see her smile at him. It was the first time since he'd met her that he had received a positive response from her. "What is it about you, Ms. Thompson, that has me ready to don armor and sword, seeking out a dragon to slay?"

She gave him a toothy grin this time. "I make you feel like that?"

He flashed an expression of disbelief. "Do not tell me you don't know about the spell you cast upon me? If you don't, you are a dangerous woman," he told her.

"Mmm-hmm, that was some smooth mackin'," she said, but loving every word.

"I don't know too much about mackin', but what I do know is that it's outlining in a poetic way the effect or description of someone. Embellishing characteristics that are already beautiful."

"No, you just didn't mack me by defining *mackin'*," she laughed. She felt greater than good now.

Octave apparently felt the same. "Gwendolyn," he began, as he reached out for her hand across the table. "I would like to get to know you more. I–"

"Ya mean, you wanna be my man?" she asked, cutting him to the chase. She was on his level and ready for whatever.

He was taken aback by her directness. "Well, yeah. Since you put it so bluntly."

"Well, yes, I would like that a lot," she said. She had on her Sasha Fierce vibe, which she called her "G-wen" vibe, as in G-win.

He squeezed her hand affectionately, wearing a grandma grin, and she squeezed his back with a winning smile.

"If I could get rid of my other problem with such ease, I'd be good. My life would be complete. I plan to take on the CEO position myself," he said.

Gwendolyn noted the committed tone in his voice and was glad she had been bold earlier. Here was a man who respected her, and one she knew wanted her. Her in totality. However, she could not stand the diffident attitude he had toward his brother, and she could not believe he did not see the obvious. But she guessed that was what a partner was for. To not only console, but to support; to point out things that your partner did not know or missed. Basically, to be a team player.

"Octave, I can't see how your brother is a problem," she began. "You are the chairman of the board, the majority stockholder, and pretty much the owner. You don't have to present your brother as a contender for the CEO position. You are in position to call his whole campaign off.

"And shoo', if you wanna be the next CEO, you should voice your intent." Gwendolyn finished, with a frown. She was not mad at him, but mad at Julien for causing her man to feel pressured.

Octave leaned back in his chair, folded his arms, then rubbed his chin, digesting Gwendolyn's words.

He'd never looked at his situation that way. He was so busy thinking of Julien as a brother instead of as a man interviewing for a job where he was the employer. Looking at things from Gwendolyn's perspective made Octave lean one shoulder back and want to bang on his chest.

He nodded. "I see," he said. "I am grateful to you Gwendolyn. You are a hell of a woman, ya know?"

"Yes, I do," she said, smiling.

He laughed and shook his head. "And," he began, leaning toward her. She leaned forward in response. "I am glad you are my woman," he said, then went in for a kiss. Their lips met with passion, and he relished the fact that he had caught a winner—a special woman. And she was relishing the fact that she had finally come into her own and embraced her womanliness.

Chapter 26

Tuesday

On the day of the second meeting, all were in attendance. Two attendees were of a different status this time around. Gwendolyn and Octave were not just a couple, they were in different businesses. Gwendolyn was the founder and CEO of GT Finance, and Octave was taking the reins of his birthright as founder in descent, controlling stockholder, chairman, and CEO of Armedia.

Julien was posted by the wall again with his sidekick lawyer, awaiting his time to take the floor. Chairman Royal, seated at the head of the table, called for order.

"Hello, everyone. I am glad you all are here, and I hope everyone had a nice weekend. I sure did," he said. "What I would like to assure you all is that I plan to let this meeting be one of expansion and improvement to secure our investment."

Everyone nodded. Octave turned to Julien. He could not help remembering their lifelong rivalry.

*   *   *

"Julien scored again!" his dad said to him. "Octave, did you see that?" he asked. How couldn't he see it when they were seated next to each other watching the same football game?

"Yeah, Daddy," little Octave said.

"Your brother's a beast on the field." Octave did not comment on that. He could not help but think his dad felt less about him because his brother was the athlete of the family while he chose to excel in academics.

In fact, Octave hated sports. Or at least he didn't care for sports like a lot of the male species did. It was a no-brainer for him. And his source of entertainment was novels.

"Let's go meet up with him," his dad said when the game was over. Octave's dad walked to the field, where Julien was getting patted on his back for the team's win. Octave watched his dad's face light up and transform into a Joker's face, for his smile stretched ear to ear.

Then his dad opened his arms and yelled, "Come here, tiger!" Little Julien threw down his helmet and ran into his dad's arms. They embraced, and his dad raised him off the ground. "That'a boy.

Over his daddy's shoulder, Julien stuck a tongue out at Octave, mouthing "Nanny nanny boo boo." He knew Octave was jealous of him for receiving all the attention from their dad. Octave responded with a middle finger. But he knew he could not outshine Julien in sports. All he could do was wear it. And Octave did time after time again.

*   *   *

But now those days were over with. He wondered if Julien would be able to wear it. Only way to find out was to see for himself.

"Mr. Royal, your request for CEO is denied," he said simply. Then turned to the others. "I am personally taking on the position myself. After further insight into an old plan, I have decided to take on the CEO position. My grandfather, Octave M. Royal the First's vision of Armedia is rooted in me, and I am passionate about seeing it through."

Julien looked in horror. "How you gonna do that, Mr. Chairman?"

"I think I made myself clear how," Octave replied. With a wink and smirk that said "Nanny nanny boo boo."

"This is an outrage. You didn't even seek the board's vote," Julien whined, then he looked to each board member. Blank faces stared back at him. Valencia rolled her eyes. "This is bullshit!" Julien exclaimed.

"Mr. Royal," Octave began in an even tone, "this is business. And your display of emotions is uncalled for and inappropriate. I suggest, if you would like to remain at this meeting as a stockholder, you get a hold of yourself."

Julien looked at Octave with an expression that would scare a lion. "Samuel, let's go," he said to his attorney. Having his lawyer there made his whole presentation seem like a joke. When had anyone ever seen Tim Cook or any other CEO come to the stage accompanied by an attorney?

Octave settled down and began to address the attendees with civil authority as his brother stormed out of the room. He looked at Gwendolyn as he spoke.

She smiled and gave him a wink. Her gesture had the effect of a Red Bull; he sat up straighter and spoke with more energy. He knew that he had a force behind him that was more motivational than a hundred Tony Dungys. The most potent natural resource was a woman. To all in the room, he seemed to be the man of the house, which was a metaphor meaning that the man is the house. He was a source of shelter and safety.

And Gwendolyn giving him that push that he needed made her the foundation of the house—and a solid foundation at that. It has been said time and time again, but few heed the saying, that "behind every strong man, there's an even stronger woman."

Octave nodded and smiled at Gwendolyn, thinking, I got me one. One meaning a strong woman.

Epilogue

Ancient Egypt

Osiris tossed and turned in his bed, then abruptly woke up in a pool of sweat. Isis was startled awake by his violent thrashing. He arose, breathing as hard as if he had run a marathon, looking frantically around the bedchamber. When reality sank in that he was in the safe confines of his bed, his breathing subsided.

"What's wrong, my god?" Isis asked him.

"I had a bad night vision," he said, although that was an understatement. He'd had the worst night vision.

Isis took a cloth off the stone table next to the peacock-feather filled bed and began wiping his face. "It is all right now," she cooed.

He looked at her with eyes that looked set to jump out their sockets. "It seemed so real," he said.

The horrible vision was clearly haunting him from the tone of his voice. Isis felt his fear. "What was your vision was about?"

"Set."

"Again?" she said, dragging out the word. Isis knew the threat that her brother-in-law imposed. But she did not understand why Set haunted her husband's night visions.

He continuously shook his head. "It seemed more vivid," he told her. A vivid vision was known to ring true; Isis knew. But—

"As vivid as the last one?" she asked incredulously. Osiris had claimed vividness before about a pestilence that never came about, not to mention his recurring visions of his brother defeating him and declaring himself ruler over Egypt, which was yet to happen.

He sensed his wife's skepticism. Maybe he was tripping, but he physically felt this vision. He'd managed to incorporate all his senses in his night vision.

Osiris got out of bed. Isis, with her beautiful saucer-big eyes, watched him. His divine undergarments were soaking wet. She peered down to see if he was dripping on the floor, but he was not. Looking at him as he stood with his back toward her, Isis could not help but wonder if each bead of sweat that seeped out of his flesh was fear being flushed out. Or was it Osiris drowning in his fear to the point that it spilled out of him?

He turned to her. His eyes were filled with worry. His thick lips were pressed hard together, as if glued. It seemed to Isis that he was intentionally pressing his mouth closed in order not to say whatever damning thought was flowing in his brain.

"Set is coming, my goddess," he declared. Isis leaned her head to the side. "I don't mean at this moment," he said, although he already knew that she was just being facetious. "But he is coming."

Isis was adept at telepathy; however, she did not have to read his mind to know what he was thinking. He was depressed and paranoid—defeated. He felt conquered even before the battle. Isis could not stand to see her husband, her god who was her sun, in such a downtrodden mood. It hurt and angered her to see him like this.

"So, when are you going to him?" Osiris frowned in question. "You speak of Set's arrival, yet you don't speak of yours," she said. She could have simply told him, "Don't just sit around and wait for your enemy's arrival. Go to him," but she wanted him to come to his own conclusion.

He considered her words, rubbing his chin.

"Might I remind you that you are god?" Isis continued. "You worry and wallow in fear as a sheep will, instead of thinking about what you can do. Osiris, my god, you are not defeated, and you have to stop thinking about what Set could do and start thinking about what you can do," she told him.

Her words resonated, and he considered tactics that he could use to rid himself of his problematic brother. All were sound and strategic maneuvers. Osiris paused, fingers still on his chin, and looked at his wife, sitting up in bed and shining like a torch. Isis's dark and lovely beauty enhanced her cunning.

But most of all, the look in her oval eyes made Osiris feel like a giant, with his head above the clouds. She didn't believe him to be anything less than powerful, adroit, and invincible, and Osiris couldn't help feeling the same about himself. She triggered something in him—that little giant within him named Will, reminding him of himself, giving him perspective and focus on that which is productive.

He moved to the bed, climbed on, and crawled to his wife. Then he kissed her passionately. His passion for her exceeded love or lust at that moment. Isis responded with equal passion, kissing him back. After a moment of intensified lovemaking, she broke away from him. The magnetic force of their desire lingered between their lips and bodies, drawing them together. However, Isis maintained her distance.

"Go handle your business," she said.

$$* \qquad * \qquad *$$

Set was on the edge of Cairo, preparing an insurgence against his brother. He had already served to have his loyal men infiltrate Osiris's army and position themselves for the ripe taking of the goddom, just as Osiris's night vision had prophesized. News of the prophecy reached Set almost immediately after Osiris awakened, for he had many spies in the pyramid.

Set walked around the camp of warriors, observing his men. They were all blacker than the darkest night, with fire-red eyes. They looked like red-eyed shadows that, if cast upon someone, their shadowing would be fatal. Like lava passing over a life and leaving only ashes. Set nodded in satisfaction at how terrifyingly strong his warriors looked.

He approached three of his trusted generals. "Tuteh, Marley, Farrah. Salute!"

"Salute!" they greeted him in unison.

"Are we ready to proceed?" he asked.

Marley and Farrah turned to Tuteh, who frequented the pyramid palace the most. He had the best knowledge to take down the god Osiris. "Yes, we are ready to move in," he said.

Set stared at him with his fiery red eyes, which Tuteh took to mean he wanted more details, for the god was meticulous in his endeavors. He continued, "Osiris slumbers at sunset, and he rises when the sun does, which gives us ample opportunity to make our move."

"The sunset, aye?" Set liked the ring to that. It had to be an omen that meant he would defeat Osiris the sun god and set himself up as the ruler of Egypt. He rubbed his chin and nodded. "We move in at dawn, then." The warriors nodded.

Epilogue II

Dawn came fast and night even faster for the rich land of Egypt. Egyptian men and male children worked the fields, the architects drew up plans for new monuments, and the historians and artists recorded the times on the many completed monuments that their work might endure for generations to come. While these Egyptians worked and sculpted for Egypt's legacy, Set and his men were in the process of making new history.

They stormed the pyramid and headed toward the bedchamber to seize Osiris in bed. Set, in a majestic purple robe, made a hand gesture indicating to his men to draw their weapons. Then he stepped back and nodded toward the closed chamber doors. The warriors charged, breaking the doors down and rushing inside.

Osiris, in bed, sat upright. "What's the meaning of this?" he declared, as the warriors flooded into the room. They swarmed around the god's bed with swords and spears. Osiris turned to his right, seeing that his wife was not there. The feeling of déjà vu hit him, but he felt more offended than anything. Osiris was furious, but the ominous pressure of the armed warriors around him was suffocating.

As his fury built, Set walked in the room. "Set, my brother, are you behind this?" Osiris asked in surprise.

"How is it that this is a surprise, my brother," Set responded, "when your vision already revealed your fate?"

Osiris recalled the vision and immediately felt the vivid foreboding associated with it. He shook his head and turned to Set, staring him in the eyes. Osiris's eyes were as fiery red as his brother's. He'd had enough with the mirror image of himself threatening and disturbing his reign.

The vision revealed that his wife, Isis, would revive him to defeat Set and reign unopposed from then on. But what good was a vision with a sweet ending when it came by way of excruciating pain and humiliation? He refused to endure either.

Osiris turned to his guards. "Seize him!" he commanded, pointing a damning finger at Set. None of the guards moved.

Set looked at the still warriors, then threw his head back and released a booming laugh. His laughter rattled the room. When he finished laughing, he looked at Osiris with contempt. "I heed visions," he said. "Especially favorable visions." Set also knew of the outcome of Osiris's vision, but considering the impossibility of it, he had no worries of his soon-to-be-mutilated brother thwarting his reign any time soon.

Osiris frowned. Set turned to Tuteh, who was next to him. "Seize him," he said. Tuteh nodded to the warriors, who abruptly turned from the bed and moved in to seize Set. They grabbed the unarmed god.

Set didn't struggle at first because he didn't realize what was happening. But when he understood that the warriors he had sent to infiltrate his brother's army to gain entry and cross Osiris were now crossing him, he fought and kicked. But it was to no avail. The guards had a death grip on him, which meant death for him was imminent.

$$* \qquad * \qquad *$$

Osiris, heeding his vision and his wife's prompting, had gone into immediate action. The guards in his vision were compromised, so he utilized his telepathic abilities to expose the traitors. This simple task proved difficult because their minds were set on serving a god who looked just like him. And much of their minds were focused on scenarios on how they could defend the god and goddom effectively.

Osiris was losing time and hope. Then he came across the stoic General Tuteh. Tuteh was one of the few warriors who did not seek attention, but he had an inquisitive eye in the god's presence. Osiris noticed and summoned Tuteh to his throne.

"Salute, my god," Tuteh greeted Osiris as he entered the room and stood before him.

Sitting straight and majestic on his throne, Osiris said, "I know you work for my brother."

Tuteh remained silent, wearing an indifferent expression. If he were called out for his treachery, he would face his fate as a warrior.

"You have set yourself up for failure. My brother Set will fail," he declared. "What has he assured you?"

Tuteh did not respond. Not out of defiance, but because Set had not promised him anything.

After a moment, Osiris said, "That's what I thought. My brother is a parasite. All he would do is take, use, and inevitably destroy. But if you side with me, Tuteh, I will make your descendants pharaohs."

Tuteh knew it was an offer he could not refuse. The god was firm in his blessings; once he declared them, it was assured. Also, Tuteh knew that if he did not accept, he would be tortured to the extent that he would wake up every day wishing he were dead. If he did die, the goddess could resurrect him to endure the torture again and again.

*   *   *

Osiris looked at his brother with a winning smile, enjoying how he had beaten his brother's cross with a double-cross.

"I, too, heed visions," he said. "One that Isis unveiled reminded me that I am the master of my own destiny." He turned to Tuteh. "Take him to the dungeon and fulfill the prophecy." Tuteh nodded to the guards.

"No!" Set yelled. "Tuteh, you can't!" The warriors began dragging him away. "We're like brothers!"

When Tuteh heard this, his eyebrows rose. Set knew he had used an improper comparison to demonstrate their allegiance as the words left his mouth. Tuteh shook his head at him.

"Nooo!" Set screamed as he was led out toward the dungeon.

Set's outcome refuted his sunset confirmation. Now when the sun sets, many know why. Osiris was so elated by the defeat of his brother that he ordered a celebration. Later that day, on top of the steps of the pyramid palace, Osiris stood before his subjects, as Isis sat on her throne to the left of his, and addressed them:

"I declare that Isis, my wife, your goddess, is the Goddess of gods because she is capable of resurrecting a god." The crowd of thousands of Egyptians roared, shouting, "IS THIS TRUE, ISIS? ARE YOU THE GODDESS OF GODS?!"

Osiris stepped back toward his wife and held out his hand. Isis took it, rising from her throne, and the goddess, with a cool, jazzy prance, came to stand at the top of the pyramid steps.

Standing at her full height in a regal, elegant pose, her slender arms were draped in jewels, and she held a bejeweled ankh in her left hand. The ankh was the genesis of the symbol for the female sex.

The subjects grew silent, an unbelievable feat with such a large crowd. Isis peered at them, as if to let them know she saw them all, and said, "I am who I am." Then she turned to take her seat again. After the goddess's words sank in, they erupted with cheers.

Isis's simple response spoke volumes. It meant that she was whomever she thought she was, and surely the people could interpret her as they saw fit. And since she did not boast of her supreme godliness, they dubbed her as such. This idea of Isis was hinted at in Ancient Egyptian mythology in that the god Amon-ra, birthed from the Nile River, had no ending, only a beginning—the God of gods. And the first badass god was Isis.

Being Ra meant she was badass. Amon-ra was often referred to by his anagram, Raamon, pronounced *woman*. So, Amon-ra, Raamon, and Isis combined to be translated in millions of languages throughout history to mean "I am woman."